Men Seek

MEN SEEKING WOMEN

Love and Sex On-line

PO BRONSON, RICHARD DOOLING, ERIC GARCIA,
PAUL HOND, GARY KRIST, DAVID LISS,
CHRIS OFFUTT, ALEXANDER PARSONS,
ROBERT ANTHONY SIEGEL, BRUCE STERLING

ATRANDOM.COM

NEW YORK

Compilation copyright © 2001 by Random House, Inc.
"Prisoners of the Heart" copyright © 2001 by Eric Garcia
"Payback Time" copyright © 2001 by Gary Krist
"No Yellers" copyright © 2001 by Chris Offutt
"Minesweeper" copyright © 2001 by David Liss
"Dante Visits Inferno Media's Online Technical-Support Forum"
copyright © 2001 by Richard Dooling
"Code" copyright © 2001 by Bruce Sterling
"The Face in the Glass" copyright © 2001 by Paul Hond
"The Risk-Reward Ratio" copyright © 2001 by Robert Anthony Siegel
"Calista X" copyright © 2001 by Alexander Parsons
"Endpoint" copyright © 2001 by Po Bronson

All rights reserved under International and Pan-American Copyright Conventions. Published, in print and electronic editions, in the United States by AtRandom.com Books, a division of Random House, Inc., New York, and simultaneously in Canada by Random House of Canada Limited, Toronto.

ATRANDOM.COM BOOKS and colophon are trademarks of Random House, Inc.

ISBN 0-8129-9167-2

Printed in the United States of America on acid-free paper
Random House website address: www.atrandom.com

2 4 6 8 9 7 5 3

First Edition

Contents

Editor's Note / Jonathan Karp   *vii*

1. Prisoners of the Heart / Eric Garcia   *3*

2. Payback Time / Gary Krist   22

3. No Yellers / Chris Offutt   *41*

4. Minesweeper / David Liss   *47*

5. Dante Visits Inferno Media's Online Technical-Support
   Forum / Richard Dooling   *75*

6. Code / Bruce Sterling   *88*

7. The Face in the Glass / Paul Hond   *104*

8. The Risk-Reward Ratio / Robert Anthony Siegel   *135*

9. Calista X / Alexander Parsons   *159*

10. Endpoint / Po Bronson   *177*

Editor's Note

Jonathan Karp

The title for this anthology of original short stories was inspired by a popular site on America Online, a realm called Love@AOL, where 680,000 men and women post personal ads. A cursory glance through "Men Looking for Women in Buffalo" reveals a typical range of entries, each one with a succinct title, from "Forever Yours" to "Italian Stallion Needs a Rider" to "Chain Me in Your Kitchen."

These postings are merely a sliver of the new sexual frontier thriving online. Chat rooms, where members assume anonymous identities and reveal many things they usually wouldn't, have long been among AOL's most frequented sites. As author Kara Swisher notes in her history of America Online, *aol.com,* the popularity of these chat rooms was a crucial factor in the company's early success. Swisher reports that AOL users spend 25 percent of their on-line time in forums such as "Black Lesbians" and "Luv Cops N Firemen," "Hot Hot Nurses," and "Romantic Millionaires."

For all that has been written about Internet culture and the New Economy, the social dimensions of technology often seem to be overlooked. When no less a personage than Rush Limbaugh can an-

nounce that he met his most recent wife through an e-mail correspondence, it becomes clear that the means of mating have changed,
that new opportunities exist, and that with those opportunities come
new questions about the way we communicate and express our most
elemental longings.

To shed light on this romantic revolution, Random House has en-
listed ten male authors to create stories from the frontier. Our only
directive to each writer was that he write a tale of love and desire online. We left the rest to them, and their contributions are as original
and distinct as their literary voices. The quest for love is eternal, but
as these stories prove, the landscape keeps changing, and even if
you don't ascribe to all of those Mars/Venus theories, it's clear that
a lot of guys can't bring themselves to ask for directions.

We hope our first e-book anthology, *Men Seeking Women,* will
serve as a guide and muse for all of the imaginations and hearts
wandering online. May your journey be a satisfying one.

—

*Jonathan Karp is a Vice President and Senior Editor at Random
House.*

Men Seeking Women

PRISONERS OF THE HEART

Eric Garcia

Ann-Marie Moore was finished with the world of men. Her last date had ended when the attorney with whom she'd been set up excused himself from the table, vanished into the café bathroom, and didn't emerge for three hours. Ann-Marie sat there the entire time, tapping her foot to the beat of the mediocre house band, staring at the double doors with murderous intensity. And when her date finally reappeared, glancing around the restaurant like a five-point buck on the first day of hunting season, he didn't respond to her calls or whistles. No, he kept on walking, past Ann-Marie, past the table, past the bar, out the front door and into the night. By the time she arrived home at her empty two-bedroom apartment at the end of the evening, her left heel broken, makeup streaked with tears, she realized that, all told, it was the best date she'd had in months.

She was thirty-five years old, carried six thousand dollars' worth of credit card debt, and owned two cats, one of which she hadn't seen in weeks. This, predictably, was the male one. She had never been to Paris, though the prior summer she had spent three miserable days in the sweltering Las Vegas heat, and she could count the number of times she'd been truly drunk on seven fingers. Her mother called her every other day, at 8:00 P.M. precisely, and the first question out of her mouth was always whether or not Ann-Marie had eaten. The next question, of course, was about her love life. Most of the time, Mother was spoon-fed a meal of beautiful lies.

For Ann-Marie had worked her way through the visible spectrum of males, finding herself deep in love and lust with men of all races and skin tones. Strong arms, strong backs, skinny legs, wide butts, caramel tones, pale faces; a smorgasbord of masculine delights. But one by one, regardless of their physical differences, regardless of their varying professions, hobbies, and personalities, each and every one of them had a single element in common, a collective trait that both identified and grouped them as members of the male gender:

They left.

At the end of the day, after the roses and the chocolates and the sweet whispers in bed, Jason and Miguel and Brian and T.J. and Elton and George and the rest of them found an escape clause in their vows of love and took off into the night. Walter flew the coop at high noon, actually, running out the front door with his jacket thrown over his shoulder, as if he were on a train platform and chasing after the 4:09 Southbound for Atlanta.

So as of Sunday night at 11:34 P.M., Ann-Marie Moore was finished with the world of men, and good riddance to them. After fifteen years of hard dating, her bank account was substantially depleted, her bedframe was cracked in three places, and her self-esteem had found a tight little hole deep down inside some gutter in which to curl up and die. It was enough, and finally, gratefully, it was over.

On Monday morning, flush with the excitement of a new, untested lifestyle, she treated herself to a bubble bath. Called in late to work, told them she had a spot of flu. She ran the hot water, submerged herself, closed her eyes, and drifted off to a world where men didn't walk out of restaurants and ignore their dates; where men didn't act like wild animals, treating women like gristle on the bone; where men were, finally, what all of the fairy tales and romance books said they were supposed to be: Men.

And for an hour and a half, it was glorious.

When the phone rang at eleven, she answered it out of habit. Realizing that she was still supposed to be ill, Ann-Marie flopped sideways in the bath, hanging her head off the edge in order to lend her voice the proper amount of nasal stuffiness. "Hello?" she said hoarsely.

"I found him."

Ann-Marie sat up quickly, water splashing onto the bathroom linoleum. "Excuse me?"

"I found him. I found the man for me." It was Ellen, always Ellen, three-phone-calls-a-day Ellen, who regularly regaled Ann-Marie with sob stories of her own sordid love life.

"What man?"

"Ulysses," she said proudly, with a hint of grandeur. "He lives upstate."

Ann-Marie stood and grabbed for a towel, balancing on her left foot as she tried to lean across the tub. The terry cloth felt good against her bare skin. "You're being vague, here, Ellen. I'm late for work."

"Forget work. Call in sick."

"I did already. I took a half day."

"Then take a full day. You must get online."

Ann-Marie clucked her tongue. Ellen was always full of demands, no matter the situation. She was barely able to start a sentence without some variation of the word *must.* "Why?"

"Because I've found paradise, darling. We've been looking in the wrong places for years. Go online as soon as possible—I'm telling you, that's where they are."

"Who?"

"The men," sighed Ellen. "All the luscious men."

—

They were in front of Ellen's computer forty minutes later, staring at the screen as the old modem dialed up a connection. "So I'm online, just messing around," Ellen explained, "bouncing from page to page, checking out links, and I hit this amazing site . . ."

Ann-Marie didn't own a computer. She hadn't ever bounced around anywhere, let alone from page to page, and didn't much care about the whole Internet craze. She thought of it as a sidebar to her life, a state of affairs that, while meaning a great deal to a certain percentage of the population, could just as easily continue its existence parallel to hers, without the two ever crossing.

But suddenly Ellen was talking about websites and search engines and pen pals and then, as if it were the most logical transition in the world, she was on to men. And she was on to Ulysses.

"I wrote him first," she said, "because that's how the rules work. You read their profiles, you find one of them that you like, and you e-mail him a message."

"So there are rules?" Already Ann-Marie was suspicious. If, as she'd decided, she was through with the world of men, then she was through with the world of men, digital or otherwise. Any extra regulations would only complicate matters further.

But Ellen was already online and typing away, slapping a URL into the location box of her browser. In the time that it took for the page to load, Ann-Marie decided that she would listen to Ellen for five minutes, then stand up from the ergonomically correct desk chair and walk out of the apartment, down to her car, and make it back to work just in time for her boss to bawl her out for missing the morning meetings.

That's when the page fully loaded, and there it was, five inches high on the seventeen-inch monitor, glaring out at Ann-Marie in a bright, gaudy, Web-design-in-a-box font, replete with whirling animation:

Prisoners4Love.com

Ann-Marie tried not to laugh. She understood that this was important to Ellen—in the way that *everything* was important to

Ellen—but it was difficult to take seriously. Below the blinking homepage title was a small cartoon prisoner in black-and-white cartoon stripes, peering out from behind small cartoon bars, a small cartoon heart beating in his small cartoon chest. *We made mistakes in life,* the caption read. *Don't make a mistake in love!*

"Armed robbery, if that's what you're thinking," said Ellen.

"They're all . . . armed robbers?"

"No, that's what Ulysses is in for. Armed robbery. But he was framed."

Ann-Marie smiled her best smile—this was her friend, after all—and grabbed her pocketbook. "It's all fascinating, Ellen," she said, "but Mr. Saponaro is gonna give me the boot if I don't get in by two—"

"Sit, sit," said Ellen, pulling Ann-Marie back into the seat. "Ten minutes. You must try it for ten minutes, and if you don't find someone fascinating, you can go."

Ann-Marie looked at her watch. If her car started properly and if traffic held up right, she could sacrifice the time and still make it into the office before the two o'clock deadline. Ellen was a kook, but she was a kind kook, and the least Ann-Marie could do was humor her for a while.

"Ten minutes?"

"No more. I swear it."

———

Six hours and three apologetic phone calls to Mr. Saponaro later, Ann-Marie was still busy searching through the Prisoners4Love website. She'd already browsed nearly a hundred profiles under the Men Seeking Women subheading, and was amazed to find that she'd scavenged her way through only 10 percent of the available male inmates.

"Ooh," squealed Ellen, "click that one, click that one."

"Raymundo Ruiz?"

"Listen to that name. Rrrraymundo," she trilled. "Rrrraymundo Rrrruiz. The things it does to my tongue . . ."

"Then you write him," Ann-Marie suggested.

"I've got Ulysses," said Ellen. She'd been going on about her new beau the whole time, showing Ann-Marie the e-mails they'd been sending back and forth for the last two weeks. Ulysses was indeed in prison for armed robbery, and, to hear him tell it, he'd been set up by the police as a result of his being the wealthiest pawnshop patron this side of the tracks. He never quite gave corroborating evidence or any logical link between the two, but Ellen believed him with all her soul, and that was all that mattered to Ann-Marie. Ulysses would be up for parole in six years. After that, said Ellen, the heart would lead the way.

Most of the prisoners' profiles read in much the same way. Name, birthdate, reason for incarceration, sob story regarding said reason, a litany of likes and dislikes, and a heartfelt plea to send e-mail, cookies, cigarettes, and such. Photographs were not allowed on the site, though the inmates went to a good deal of trouble describing themselves in intimate detail. Ann-Marie was skeptical of all their claims, partially because of their incarceration, but more so because of the sheer fact that they were proud owners of penises. But she stuck it out because, after the first thirty minutes of searching, Ann-Marie suddenly realized that despite their genetic inadequacies, the men on the Prisoners4Love website had one inhibiting factor that had never held back the men in the free world:

They couldn't run away.

And this made them fantastically attractive.

"Try that one!" Ellen said, pointing a manicured nail at the screen. "Claude."

"No last name," mumbled Ann-Marie. "Why's that?"

"Who cares? It's all the more mysterious that way."

Ann-Marie shrugged and clicked on Claude's name. The main page disappeared, the lights on the 56K went wild, and a stream of letters poured onto the screen.

My name is Claude, the new page read, *and I am a prisoner of the state. More important, I am a prisoner of the heart.*

Cheesy standard intro. Must be some sort of form opening they discuss in the mess hall. But Ann-Marie read on.

I understand what it is to be without choice. I understand what it is to be without hope. And I understand what it is to be without love. This is what defines me today, in here, but I know, out there, that it defines you, as well.

For there are those who will treat women as if they were possessions, to be discarded along with the refuse. I will never do this. There are those who will get what they want and then vanish like the morning mist. I will always stay. I am the boat, and you are the rock to which I wish to attach myself. Your love is the port in my storm.

But I am more than flowery words on a computer screen. I am flesh and blood, locked up because of my intellectual beliefs, because of my voice. More than anything else, I seek companionship, a woman with whom to share my thoughts and feelings, and, more important, a woman who wishes to share her thoughts and feelings with me.

I seek an equal, a partner. A lover of life, and a lifer in love. Please, if you are this special woman, hear my plea and write me back.

Claude.

"Oooh, I like him. Try it," Ellen suggested.

Ann-Marie wasn't convinced. "I don't know . . ."

"What's the worst that could happen?"

"He gets angry, breaks out of prison, finds a hunting knife, and tracks me down."

"Okay," said Ellen, "but he'll probably buy you dinner first."

Ann-Marie's e-mail to Claude was short and, she felt, rather impersonal. That was how she wanted it, at least to start. She gave her first name only, just as he had, and listed very little about her life. Instead, she wrote out a laundry list of qualities that she found unacceptable in a mate, and hoped that he wouldn't have too many of them.

Claude's answer came back within an hour. *Ann-Marie,* he wrote, *I am pleased to make your acquaintance, and I hope that we will be-*

come fast friends. Regarding your list of negative qualities, I am glad to say that as of this moment, I am free of all but one: I have indeed seen a number of Clint Eastwood movies—here in prison, in fact— but rest assured that I am much more a fan of Every Which Way But Loose *than, say,* Dirty Harry. *I hope this is to your satisfaction.*

And it was.

———

Over the next three weeks, Ann-Marie logged in more than fifty e-mails from Claude, sending return letters across the electronic void as often and as quickly as possible. Much of her time at home was taken up at the WebTV system she'd purchased, sitting in front of her twenty-one-inch television, typing away as fast as her fingers would allow. At work, Ann-Marie finagled her way onto a computer linked to the office T1 connection, prompting Mr. Saponaro to congratulate her on her initiative. Now that she was gaining computer skills, he said, she'd be eligible for promotion. Ann-Marie smiled and thanked him, but didn't care about moving up the company ladder; she just wanted access to the e-mail server.

It began, as many of her prior relationships had, with the small things, the superficial aspects of their lives. Ann-Marie's favorite foods, colors, television shows—chicken curry, magenta, *Alice* reruns. The way Claude brushed his hair when he was allowed grooming utensils, how he stared out at the sunlight through the bars, watching it stream past the prison walls. It was the kind of idle chitchat that usually took up space on a first date if the waiter was slow bringing the food. But as their relationship matured, so did the meat of their conversations.

Claude, she learned, was a radical in his youth, an intellectual whose ideas about the government and its secret projects threw a monkey wrench of fear into the workings of the establishment. He described himself as an innocent who was thrust into the world of knowledge, an untamed beast who was suddenly trained and educated, and therefore had a moral imperative to train and educate others. More than once, he referred to the Tarzan legend, though

Ann-Marie never quite saw the connection. In any case, his outspoken views on everything from the Kennedy assassination to secret underground labs and genetic engineering were viewed as subversive and dangerous and not to be tolerated.

So they locked him in a cage and threw away the key. No privileges, no visitors. The prison warden and jailers had no idea Claude was even on the computer; he used it on the sly, logging on whenever and wherever he got the chance. If they let him into the yard for some playtime, for example, he managed to sneak in a few sentences on his way out of the building, and a few more on his way back in. One time, the warden caught him staring up at the CRT, typing away, and he was sent to a room in the basement where they administered grueling shock therapy for two hours straight.

Ann-Marie wanted to write the prison board about the abuses to which Claude had been subjected, but he was adamant that she stay silent. *We cannot seek justice from the ones who dispense injustice,* he wrote. *You and I, we shall have our day together in the sun, and then, and only then, shall we both swing free.*

She just loved it when he talked like that.

They discussed art and politics and music and travel, all of it shunted through Prisoners4Love.com, all of it magical and special and filled with the kind of banter that only two equals can share. It was easy, Ann-Marie found, to open herself up to this stranger, this Claude, partially because the rapid-fire e-mail was a faceless form of communication, but mostly because he was closer to human than any other man she'd ever met. He was kind, he was funny, he was caring and decent, and most of all, he listened. He asked questions. Claude was the kind of man her mother had always talked about, and even if he wasn't quite a gallant knight in shining armor, he was at least a kindly knave in not-too-soiled trousers.

And he was sensitive, there was no doubt about that, too soft a soul for the rigors of prison life. *My fellow inmates are little more than animals,* he wrote to Ann-Marie one day. *A convict named Albert is imprisoned next to me, and some days we converse through the bars. But he understands little of what I say, and I choose to un-*

derstand little of his grunts and groans. Most of the time, he sits in the corner of his cell and pleasures himself. I imagine his crime must be great, indeed. Across the way is Pierre, and he regularly enrages our jailers by throwing his feces at them through the bars; he finds this the height of amusement, and the more I tell him to refrain, the more often he does it. Animals surround me, and nothing more. But I was once exactly like them, a savage in a world of innocents, and I can only hope that one day they, too, will feel the warm glow of enlightenment.

Ann-Marie responded in kind, writing of her coworkers, of her boss, of the details of her workaday life, and though no one on her side of the bars threw feces or masturbated in public, she managed to make their trials and tribulations with company bureaucracy sound interesting nevertheless. And as the weeks of communication grew into months, she found herself opening up doors she thought were sealed shut long ago. She told him about the relationships she'd had with other men, about the ways in which they'd treated her. About the abuse and the heartache. *It sounds corny,* she typed, *but I think my sense of trust is gone. I think I've forgotten how to trust men.*

Do you trust me? Claude wrote back.

She didn't e-mail him for two days. Didn't want to say the wrong thing. Didn't want to say the right thing, either. For forty-eight hours she thought about his question. Was it possible to trust a man she'd never met? To trust someone whose picture she'd never seen? Whose last name she'd never even heard?

Yes, she wrote finally. *I trust you.*

And do you love me? Claude e-mailed in return.

This one took longer. By this point, Ellen's Ulysses had been freed from prison on a technicality, and the two had taken off on a whirlwind tour of Ohio, each professing to be madly in love with the other. They'd all gone out to dinner one night after he was freed but before the vacation began so that Ann-Marie could meet Ellen's new beau, and she had to admit to herself that, felony conviction aside, he seemed like quite a catch.

". . . so the fingerprints couldn't have been his," Ellen said that night, speaking with near-religious fervor. "The crime lab was in on the setup the whole time, and Ulysses's lawyers figured it out, so—"

Ulysses laid a thick hand over Ellen's shoulder, cooling her off. "It ain't important, baby," he said in a deep, gravelly tone that sent chills up Ann-Marie's legs. "We got each other now, and that's all that matters." They fell into a deep kiss that lasted over five minutes, Ann-Marie twiddling her fingers and trying to stare at the walls. But she couldn't blame them for their passion; Ulysses's retrial wasn't scheduled for two months, and the whole wide state was in front of them, ready to be conquered by their love.

So Ann-Marie didn't know if it was truly possible to fall in love over the computer, but she couldn't deny the emotion between Ellen and Ulysses any more than she could deny the deep tugs she felt on her own heart every time she saw a new e-mail appearing in her inbox. There could only be one true answer.

Yes, Claude, she wrote him after a weeklong hiatus of introspection. *Yes, Claude, I love you.*

Wonderful, was his reply. *Then marry me.*

———

Father Flaherty from www.findapriest.com presided over a beautiful ceremony, held on the virtual grounds of the website for St. Basil's Cathedral. Ann-Marie found the site, a sprawling thirty-eight pages boasting pictures of gardens, gazebos, and flowered trellises, after an exhaustive hunt that practically shut down every search engine she encountered. She even contacted the I.T. manager at the cathedral offices and convinced him to add some lace-and-rose clip art to the chapel's main page, further customizing the site for their big day.

Claude spent his time bribing and sucking up to the guards so that they'd turn their backs during the twenty-minute wedding, allowing him to hop out of the cell and log on to the chat area at the same time as Ann-Marie and Father Flaherty. There was only one invited guest—Ellen logged in from Cleveland, where she and Ulysses had taken up residence in a Traveller's Inn motel during the last few days before his new trial would begin.

Ann-Marie was alone in her house when the wedding was set to start, standing in front of her television screen, four-hundred-dollar wedding gown draped across her small frame as she typed upon the small WebTV keyboard. Traffic was heavy that day, and the static on her phone line was acting up again, making connection difficult. Ann-Marie cursed under her breath and retried the connection; she knew that Claude would only be able to log on for a maximum of twenty minutes, and after that, he'd have to return to his cell. Ann-Marie simply couldn't be late for her own wedding.

But the third dial-up did the trick, and soon she was pulling up her bookmarks and sliding into StBasilsCathedral.org, firing up her IRC chat as soon as she saw the page hit her screen. Anxiety and anticipation flew into her chest, her heart fluttering, heels digging into her living room carpet, as the communication software pulled itself into a half-screen window.

Claude was already there, and he shot her a smiley-faced emoticon. She tossed one back, fingers trembling against the keyboard. Ellen typed out *G-A-G,* and the show was on. Father Flaherty began with a sermon on truth and love, skipped over the part about natural law, and ended up with honesty and forgiveness. There were some fake cries of protest from Ellen and Ulysses and a minor incident with a fifteen-year-old who stumbled into the chat room while trying to locate his girlfriend from Norway, but soon enough Ann-Marie and Claude were typing in their vows and their "I do"s and blowing kissy-kissys across cyberspace in the form of little JPEG images Ann-Marie had yanked from some porn site. Soon enough, they were husband and wife, and, at thirty-five years of age, Ann-Marie was finally married to the greatest man she could ever imagine.

The honeymoon four days later was a two-hour affair, graciously hosted by Jamaicanvacations.com, and they provided all the MP3 and JPEG files that the two lovers would need to make their vacation complete. Ann-Marie changed from her wedding dress into a monokini she'd bought specifically for the occasion, and though the temperature outside her house was well below fifty degrees, she was on fire as she sat on her sofa in that skimpy outfit and typed steamy sentences of love to her new husband while photos of a blue ocean and perfect sky floated by on her color TV.

Their marriage was valid only in a small county up in northern Minnesota, but Ann-Marie didn't care. She loved being married to Claude, even if he didn't have a last name, and their relationship only grew more intense with every passing day. Ann-Marie found herself taking time off work in order to stay home and sew sheets and pillowcases for the day when they could truly take to the marital bed, though she had no idea of when that day might come. Claude told Ann-Marie that as part of the special prison system in which he was an inmate, parole dates were not made available to the prisoners. He had no way of knowing when he would be released, if ever. And the time away from Ann-Marie, difficult before, was now growing impossible to bear.

I grow tired of this life, he wrote one day. *Of the sterile white walls, of my jailers and their patronizing tones, of the beasts with whom I have to share my space, every day, in every way, of the pain and the tests and the terrible inhuman tortures I and my fellow inmates are forced to endure. But as long as I know that you are on the other side of these walls, my beautiful Ann-Marie, waiting for me with open arms and a smile upon that tender face, then I may indeed last an eternity, with only your letters and my dreams to see me through.*

Such optimism did not last long, and Ann-Marie's e-mails to the Department of Corrections about the abuses did no good; they either claimed not to know what she was talking about or bounced her back and forth to different departments until she gave up in frustration.

Then one night, as Ann-Marie returned from a long quarter-day at the office, she found a short e-mail in her inbox. It was from Claude, and bore none of his usual devotions of love.

They took Albert away this afternoon, it read, *I don't know where to. But when he came back, he was dying. An hour ago, as I reached through the bars and held his head in my hands, he looked up at the ceiling, smiled, and passed away. I fear that I am next.*

Ann-Marie wrote six e-mails that night, and ten the next morning, but there was no response from Claude. Another fifteen followed, and twenty more after that; she hoped that if she could flood the server with mail, *someone* would notice, *someone* would alert the proper authorities. He couldn't be dying. He couldn't be dead. This was Claude, her husband. This was the only man she had ever truly loved.

Three days later, when she had just about abandoned hope in the Internet and prepared to make an actual phone call, the telltale *bing!* of incoming mail interrupted her Web surfing. She could almost hear Claude's voice as she read the letter, his hurried, impassioned tone:

Dear one,

This is the hardest letter I have ever had to write to you, and I only wish that it did not have to be so terse. But my time is short, and you must believe me when I say all will be explained in time. For now, you need only know this: They are coming for me.

After Albert's death, Pierre was next. Last night, Enrico passed into the great beyond, and as I write this, old Ben sits behind his bars, coughing and wheezing, barely able to take a breath. My jailers tell me that nothing is wrong, that I'm being paranoid, that it's just a virus going around the prison, and that I'm safe from harm, but I know the truth. They are waiting for me, because I am the brightest, because I know it is coming, but they will indeed take me soon, and it will all be over.

Attached to this e-mail you will find an address, a blueprint, and a set of instructions. The address is that of the prison in which I am held captive; the blueprint is an exact diagram of my building. The instructions go into details regarding the date, the time, and the best method of executing the plan.

Please, my love, my life, my wife, my dearest Ann-Marie, help me. Release me from this dungeon, this hell, before they release me first.

No more letters, my love, lest they find our communications in their pitifully small disk cache. But I know that you will understand, that you will believe, and that I will see you soon. And then we will finally be together, as near to man and wife as is possible in this crazy, mixed-up world.

Your ever-faithful, ever-loving husband, Claude.

This time, it didn't take any thought on Ann-Marie's part. There was only one option, and nothing more. The law and morality and ethics would have to be put aside—none of it mattered, not now, not like this. As far as she was concerned, Claude was no different from that Hurricane Carter, whose story she'd just seen in a movie on pay-per-view—hate had put him into prison, but love, in the guise of Ann-Marie and a set of blueprints, was gonna bust him out.

—

Ann-Marie had the cab drop her off a mile from the prison so that she couldn't be placed at the scene afterward. This was the kind of thing Claude had suggested in his e-mail attachment. She also wore a wig purchased at a shop near her home, as well as an all-black ensemble picked up at an army surplus store, with the exception of her shoes, which were a pair of comfortable Nine West flats she'd had for some time. Claude had suggested that she don something easy on the feet; he said that jailbreaks tend to go awry when you dandy up the footwear.

Whatever part of her once understood and obeyed the law had been overshadowed by her desire to free her husband from danger. And even as she stood in the shadow of his prison, the cold night drilling into her clothing, chilling her skin, she felt no fear. She felt only excitement and exuberance that she and her one true love would soon be united.

Claude had already alerted her that there would be no barbed wire, no guards in high towers with powerful rifles, none of the standard things she'd naturally come to expect from a prison due to years of overexposure to film and television. But she wasn't expecting to find a short, squat building with a host of large windows along the side and a wide expanse of green lawn out front. Strong halogen lights kept it lit even in the dark of night, but it didn't have the menacing aura Ann-Marie expected. It looked a lot like the high-tech campuses she'd seen on the late-night news shows, or some low-rent college. Perhaps Claude was being held in another wing.

But despite the lack of ambient danger, she kept to the shadows as she crept up to the building, slinking around back where Claude said he'd bribed a guard to leave the door unlocked. Ann-Marie tried the knob, and was relieved to find that it was indeed open. Keeping her movements even, she pulled the door ajar and slipped inside.

Once again, her assumptions failed her. Here were stark white walls, a hallway full of doors rather than the dull gray bars her mind had conjured up. Here were signs saying DID YOU SIGN IN TODAY? and A STEADY TECHNOLOGY FOR A STEADY TOMORROW. Ann-Marie ignored it all. Set her mind to the task. Followed that blueprint.

As she walked down the empty halls, her footfalls echoing even with those comfortable flats, she kept an eye out for cell 242. Claude had said that the outer door would be open, but that once inside, he could instruct her on how to free him from behind the bars that had so long held him captive.

Ann-Marie came to an intersection of hallways and stopped to get her bearings. Suddenly, as she stared down at the printed-out map in her hands—she'd had to borrow Ellen's printer for the occasion—a voice rang out behind her, carried upon a breath tinged with filtered Marlboros.

"You're lost?"

Suddenly, Ann-Marie couldn't breathe. All of the bravado, the overriding sense of righteousness, disappeared in a lick of smoke and two simple words. It came again. "I said, are you lost? You're lookin' at that damn map like it's the Bible."

Ann-Marie turned to find a tall man draped in a white lab coat. "My husband . . ." was all she could say. She knew she was done for; no need to start lying now. The arrest would come now, followed by a quick trial and her own incarceration. Perhaps she could get off in five or six years with good behavior.

"Your husband . . . what? You're here to see him?"

Ann-Marie nodded mutely. "Two-forty-two," she mumbled.

The man sighed, grabbed her shoulders, faced her in the opposite direction, and said, "Walk. Six doors down on your right." He then brushed past her and disappeared into another room, muttering, "I don't know why they let these people inside . . ."

Ann-Marie's heart had barely swung back into a steady rhythm by the time she arrived in front of cell 242, and the proximity to her one true love made it kick up once again. She put her hand on the knob, steeling herself for the initial view, that very first glance. Ann-Marie was at the door to cell 242, but she knew that, in many ways, she was at the door to the rest of her life. And all she had to do was open it up and walk inside.

It was bright, brighter than the hallway, brighter than the halogen lights outside. Ann-Marie had to squint in order to make out the contents, and as she stepped inside, closing the door behind her, she was once again surprised at the physical makeup of the cell. Shiny metal tables were bolted to the floor, and atop them were computers, instruments, and wires that fed through loops and hooks hanging from the ceiling. Charts and tables lined the walls, graphs splattered with reds and blues, greens and oranges, as if a five-year-old with a bucket of paints had gotten to them.

And in the far corner, surrounded by a host of empty cages, was a single, five-foot-by-five-foot-by-five-foot barred cell. Attached to the front was a brass nameplate, etched with six simple letters: CLAUDE.

Ann-Marie, her brain in a fog, her body acting on its own accord, ran her fingers over the nameplate once, twice, a third time, only then bending down to take a look at her husband and true love inside his confines.

And the chimpanzee inside the cage grinned back with delight.

As Ann-Marie moved in closer, the chimp held out a sheet of paper, his furry fingers grasping the edges tightly. Ann-Marie took it from his hand, nearly tearing the letter as she snatched it away.

My dear one, it read. *If you are reading this, we are together at last. Unfortunately, my primitive vocal cords are unable to convey the words I wish to say, though my jailers here have, indeed, taught me how to type as part of their little experiment. Please, find the keys to my cage inside the closet across the room and free me, and we can run away from this place, together forever. Look into my eyes, Ann-Marie, and tell me that we will always be together.*

Ann Marie looked down at the letter, then back up at Claude, who was busily swinging from the ceiling bars in his cage. On the wall above him was a sign reading GENETIC ENGINEERING PROJECT #5C, TEST PATIENT CLAUDE. "You . . . you typed this earlier?" she asked.

Claude dropped to the floor and waddled to the front of his cell, reaching out his hands, grabbing Ann-Marie's arm in his. They stayed that way for some time, staring at each other, Claude holding her hand tightly, warming her body with his fur. He smiled widely, his sharp canines poking down past his gums.

And as she looked into those eyes, those brown globules shining back at her, she saw the love she had never before seen in a man's eyes. She saw the commitment buried deep within him, and she saw the fierce intelligence that had drawn her to his side in the first place. This was the male for whom she'd been searching all her life, only slightly fuzzier than in her dreams.

So he was shaggy, he was drooling, he had lips larger than his ears, and he probably had a shorter natural life span than most men she'd previously dated, but he was Claude, and he was her husband, and, most of all, she loved him.

Their kiss was beautiful, and Ann-Marie barely felt the slobber.

The keys were an easy matter—right there on the wall, hanging down for anyone to grab—and the cell popped open with a refreshing click. Claude jumped into her arms, his mouth slavering all over her face, and Ann-Marie staggered back from the sudden weight. But she laughed as Claude's lips spread wide in an approximation of a chortle, and she knew that everything was finally going to be okay. Mother would be happy. Father would understand, in time. And the world, if they had a problem with it, could summarily screw themselves. Let Ellen have her Ulysses. Ann-Marie had her Claude.

But on the way out of room 242, as she poked her head out the door to check for the other scientists—Claude right behind her, holding her hand, waddling along as best as his short bowlegs could carry him—Ann-Marie noticed a leash and collar sitting on one of the lab tables, and in a moment of impulse, stuffed the whole thing into her purse.

Just in case, she told herself. *Just in case.* Ann-Marie Moore had finally found herself a male, and this one wasn't getting away.

PAYBACK TIME

Gary Krist

On July 19, when Osiris Software came in with second-quarter results three cents better than Street expectations, I thought I might be in love. Osiris was one of three Nasdaq small-cap issues I'd been following on the message boards for months. The company made a software program called dIsis, which the prospectus listed as "a turnkey integrated software platform facilitating the creation of customized Internet appliances." To tell you the truth, I was never exactly sure what that meant (I first thought it had something to do with programming VCRs so you could control them via the Web), but the stock was a rocket, moving 5, 10, even 20 percent from one day to the next. I started trading it mainly because Osiris was the name of my girlfriend's cat.

Anyway, with the positive earnings surprise, shares were up four-and-change by the regular market close on July 20. I was long the stock two thousand shares, which meant that I made eight thousand dollars that day—enough to replace my old IBM ThinkPad and consider getting laser surgery to correct my lousy eyesight. And it was all because of Terra Incognita.

"Terra, baby," I posted on the Osiris message board that night. "I don't know what to say. I'm speechless with gratitude."

She replied within a half hour: "hey, just doin' my part to make y'all rich. ;)"

Octogon7, another regular who'd gone long on Terra's bullishness, oozed his admiration: "T.I., how do you always KNOW??"

"that's my little secret," she answered. Then she posted the public toll-free number for a recording of the shareholder conference call.

We were, to put it mildly, in her debt. Terra Incognita was our source, our gold mine, our inspiration. She first showed up on the Osiris board in early spring. I liked her from the beginning. It was obvious that she did her homework, but she wasn't one of those arrogant show-offs who typically commandeer the tech-stock message boards. She admitted that she didn't understand the product from a technical standpoint (who did?), but she obviously followed the company's press releases and analysts' reports. She had scoped out the competition and knew where they were on the time line toward product launch. And best of all, she had no problem sharing her wisdom with all and sundry on the message board.

I wasn't used to this kind of treatment. Just before Christmas, my longtime girlfriend Laura—the one with the cat named Osiris—had moved from Washington to take her dream job with a small production company in L.A., leaving me with her half of the rent to pay. My own supposed dream was to become an architect, to build stadiums and sports complexes for Olympic-style events, but it was a dream on hold until I could get together enough money for grad school. Meanwhile, I was stuck at an incredibly banal job editing an in-house journal for the Department of Housing and Urban Development. With one or two exceptions, I hated everybody I worked with, most of whom were middle-aged career federal employee types—the kind who wore bow ties and ate cheese sandwiches at their desks for lunch. The pay was lousy and the working environment Kafkaesque. I was miserable enough to consider moving to L.A. myself—except that Laura never asked me to.

Trading was something I'd been doing on and off for about two years, ever since my grandmother in Bethesda died and left me a thousand shares of GM. I considered myself a position trader as opposed to a day trader, which meant that I bought real companies whose stories I believed in and then actually held on to the shares for days, weeks, or even months. Thanks to Uncle Sam's lenient hours, I could usually arrange to leave work by 3:00 P.M. and get home in time to make a few trades before the closing bell; other days I just brought my laptop to work and traded during lunch hour. And it worked out pretty well. Some months I made almost as much on the market as I did at HUD.

Then Terra Incognita came into my life: "hey, anybody hear about a possible deal with totura electronics?" This post went up on a Monday in early March. It was, as far as I could tell, her first appearance on the board. And it created a stir:

Deal? Deal?? Do tell. Totura would be a major coup. 2nd largest IA producer in Japan
   —visigoth9

you mean "deal" as in buying a stake in Osiris or "deal" as in commitment to buy the platform?
   —My2Bits

the latter
   —Terra Incognita

BULLSHIT ALERT!!! t.i., you're new here. can you give source, or is this just unsubst. rumor??
   —Phil-R-Up

my sources are good, but will have to remain nameless.
   —Terra Incognita

yeahyeahyeah. who are you, and why should we believe you??
   —Phil-R-Up

She never replied, and everybody assumed that she was just another jerk trying to drive up the share price. But then, three days later, Osiris put out a press release announcing a three-year licensing agreement with Totura. The stock reacted by jumping 18.8 percent in a day.

> told you so.
> —Terra

Suddenly, Terra Incognita had our attention:

> you can't see me, t.i., but I'm groveling in the dirt right now. humblest apologies for ever doubting you.
> —Phil-R-Up

> terra!!!! your great!!!!!!!!!!!!
> —AxelBroder

> We are in awe of you, terrawoman, and await your further commands.
> —Jay3000

That was when I looked up her profile. It was pretty bare—no real name, no e-mail address, no favorite stocks or favorite books or favorite quote. Under hobbies, she had listed one thing: social work.

I wrote a private e-mail to visigoth9, a.k.a. Warren Enright, a guy I knew electronically from a couple of other stock boards. He worked for a medical supply company in Chicago and was constantly giving me dubious tips on biotechs. "So what do you think?" I wrote. "You think she works for the company?"

He answered right away. "Not likely. She'd be putting her job in jeopardy, and for what? Probably she got a one-time friend-of-a-friend piece of insider intelligence. We'll never hear from her again."

But Warren, as per usual, was wrong. Over the next few weeks, Terra became a regular poster. And she was always pretty damned impressive:

don't be fooled by the 1Q drop in marketing costs, guys. major change in strategy. before, they were going for end-consumers. now marketing focus is on trade shows and direct selling to IA manufacturers. more bang for the marketing buck that way.
—Terra

That one I hopped on myself:

Excuse my single-mindedness, T., but you'll have to translate. Are you telling us to buy or sell?
—HUDDITE

i'm not saying either one. just a little enlightenment fyi.
—Terra
p.s. don't apologize, i like single-mindedness in men. it's one of those charming characteristics you all share with dogs. (and i LOVE dogs.)

Dear Terra:
Arf! Arf!
—Jay3000

I wrote another e-mail to Warren: "I just don't get it. Why is she being so fucking *nice*? I mean, what's in it for her?"

"Peter, haven't I explained to you the concept of reciprocal altruism?" The summer before, Warren had read a few books about evolutionary psychology, so now he was an expert on human nature. "She engages in knowledge-sharing behavior because she knows, consciously or unconsciously, that she'll eventually benefit from the same kind of behavior in others."

This pissed me off. "Bullshit! She won't benefit, at least not on THIS loser board. Come on, Warren, before Terra, did anyone ever post any news that wasn't already factored into the stock price?"

His answer shot back: "Okay then, what if she's setting us up? We all learn to slavishly follow her advice, then one day she posts some bogus news about a takeover bid or something, so we all buy like fiends and drive the price up. She sells at a huge profit. Meanwhile we wait for news that never comes. Stock price sinks again, and she buys at the lower price. Classic manipulation."

This was possible, I thought, but I didn't want to admit as much to Warren. Besides, I couldn't bring myself to believe it. Terra just didn't seem like the type.

That night, after getting back from a very depressing dinner with my mother and my hotshot-lawyer brother (don't ask), I found a message from Laura on my answering machine:

"Hey, Peter, it's been a while since we talked. Guess what? I got a raise! Twenty dollars a week! Big deal, right? Anyway, call me. Osiris misses you. He misses the way you used to scratch that nick in his left ear. I miss that too. Bye."

I thought about calling her back, but it was late, and after all the wine I'd drunk in self-defense at dinner, I was beat. So I just erased the message and went straight to bed.

———

Over the next few days, the Osiris message board was humming:

hey, t.i., why don't you post your real name and phone #? at very least, e-mail address?
—hi-tek

sorry, hi. no way. a girl's gotta be careful.
—Terra

Please tell us you're not a 56-yr-old man with dimpled thighs and lots of body hair.
—eddiehaskell

i'm not a 56-yr-old man with dimpled thighs and lots of body hair.
—T.

are you a 56-year-old man WITHOUT dimpled thighs and lots of
body hair??
　—prozacboy

look, i am 100% female, 100% under-forty, and 100% uncomfortable with this line of questioning. can we please talk about the
prospects for a 1Q earnings warning next week?

I read this exchange late on a Thursday night, sitting in my dark
living room, watching little winged bugs crisscross the glowing blue
glass of the monitor. I was supposed to be editing a journal piece on
the falling number of federally subsidized housing units in major
urban areas, but I couldn't bring myself to open the file. I kept thinking about this Terra. I imagined her as tall, athletic, from somewhere
in the Deep South. She'd be appealing, but not fantasy-beautiful. A
crooked nose, maybe; a wry expression. With an adoring dog—a
mutt, say—watching her every move at the computer.

I opened an e-mail window:

Dear Laura:
　Hey, got your message. How goes the new job/new life?
Things are OK here. Washington is doing its usual spring thing—
lots of flowering trees, azaleas, etc. etc. Work at HUD? Don't ask.
I'm supposed to be editing something right now, but I'm procras-
tinating. Not that writing to you is just a form of procrastination.
I miss you, too. Do you know how long it's been since I touched
a woman's <DELETE> <DELETE> <DELETE>

I shut down the computer, took an Ambien, and fell asleep on the
couch watching Conan.

It was about a week later that Terra turned Cassandra:

bad news, guys. word is that 1Q revenues are gonna be down, repeat DOWN. expenses were down too, so actual earnings (i.e.
loss per share) could be in line w/consensus, but the street isn't
gonna like it. please protect yourselves.

This post went up at a little before 5:00 P.M.—after the regular close, but not too late to sell in the after-hours markets. Within minutes, I got an e-mail from Warren:

> This is it, Pedro. This is the set-up. She's probably sold short a shitload. Watch the stock sink on this rumor, then she'll buy at bargain prices and wait for the stock to soar again when earnings are announced on Thursday and they're totally kickass. Mark my words, boyo, and DON'T FALL FOR IT!!
> —Warren

I hesitated, I really did. I reread Terra's post three times. I was long 1,500 shares. News like this could easily shave six points off the price. I could lose almost ten thousand dollars if I didn't trust her and she turned out to be right. On the other hand, if I *did* trust her and it turned out that she was just doing a head fake, I could miss out on a big run-up. But I just couldn't see Terra doing that to us.

I logged on to my brokerage account. Osiris was already down a point and a quarter from the regular close, on heavy volume. Panicking, I dumped as much as I could, in two-hundred-share lots. By the end of the after-hours session, I'd managed to unload 1,200 shares at various prices ranging from 18⅜ to 17⅛. And I wasn't alone:

> ok, t.i., I sold it all, mostly at a loss. hate to be disloyal to old osiris, but nasdaq ain't no charity bazaar.
> —hawk71

> I went short 2K shares. Terra, gal, you better be right.
> —Intel-Inside

> No disrespect, everybody, but this is caveat-emptor land. If they knew revenues were gonna be down, wouldn't management pre-announce a warning? N'est-ce pas, Terra?
> —visigoth9

She didn't answer—not that night and not for the next few days. Meanwhile, Osiris recovered, hitting 18 on Tuesday, 19¼ on Wednesday, and 21 by midday on Thursday. I still had my last three hundred shares, and was starting to have doubts after numerous skeptical e-mails from Warren.

"Hey, Peter, it's Laura. Are you on vacation or something? I should call your mother and find out. Anyway, nothing in particular to impart. The other day I met somebody who was teaching at UCLA. He said they had a pretty decent architecture department over there. Thought you might be interested. Okay, call me."

I was at home, watching CNBC, when Osiris earnings were announced after the close on Thursday. The results were more or less just what Terra had predicted: Revenues were down 20 percent from the year-ago period, and the net loss per share was a penny worse than the First Call consensus. The stock, needless to say, was massacred in after-hours trading.

> o ye of little faith
> —Terra

I wrote in myself this time:

> So do we buy now, on the bad news? Acc. to CNBC, management claims the revenue dip is just a one-quarter anomaly. Terra, your thoughts?
> —HUDDITE

She answered right away, and even used my name this time:

> huddite, you know I don't give investment advice. but this reaction seems overdone. next few days will be rough, but I think osiris is longterm attractive at anything under 16 or 17.

Next day, I bought back my 1,200 shares, and 500 more, at the price of 11⅝.

Peter:
So sue me, I was wrong.
　—Warren

Having saved our collective asses, Terra began to attain mythic status on the board. Early in May, somebody even started an "I Love Terra" message thread (typical post: eddiehaskell: "we need a picture, terra. have pity on us. WE NEED TO SEE YOU!!!) Meanwhile, speculation about her became rampant. Everybody had his own ideas about who she was and how she knew what she knew. Intel-Inside thought she might be some Russian cleaning lady who emptied Osiris's garbage every night. Skidmarc was convinced she was the sixteen-year-old wunderkind daughter of CEO Lance Osborne. prozacboy said he'd accept Skidmarc's explanation, but he wanted her to be fourteen, not sixteen, with a short skirt and long, skinny legs. ("Take it to alt.pervert, asshole," Jay3000 told him.) Meanwhile, My2Bits (who had always seemed like the dad of the message board group) wrote: "Hey, maybe she's just a smart savvy investor who knows her stuff, ever think of that, gentlemen?"

To her credit, Terra ignored this particular discussion thread. And through late spring and early summer—as Osiris's share price struggled in a trading range of 11 to 17—she just kept giving and giving and giving:

re today's WSJ piece on burn rates: even burning 5-6M per Q, osiris has enough cash on hand to go 12 or 13 Qs; meanwhile insider buying is strong (see figures on yahoo-finance). plus, release of dIsis 2.2 should help short-term revenues.
　—Terra

gee, we love it when you talk dirty to us.
　—the reverend charles

Then, in early July, I had a dream about her. It wasn't a dream, really—just a fragment—but it was vivid. The two of us were in a canoe. I was in the stern; she was turned away from me in the bow, looking ahead. We were on a lake—Kitchamee Lake in northern Minnesota, where I used to spend summers as a kid. It was getting dark. The surface of the water was like a membrane, flat and unbroken, and there were submerged reeds everywhere that hissed as we passed through them. Bats swooped all around us, squeaking weirdly into my ears. "Terra," I said. "Don't you think we should go back? It's late." She didn't answer, but I could feel her ahead of me in the twilight. "Terra?" I said. "Terra?"

And that was it. The dream ended there. But even so, I got up the next morning and couldn't shake the dream from my head for hours.

"Hello, Peter? It's Laura. Pick up if you're there. Peter? Okay, try me later."

Terra posted later that day:

> earnings season again, guys. first call estimates a .08 loss/share. whisper number is .07/share. imho, both are too pessimistic. I hear management expects to be profitable by 1Q next year.

This time I didn't even hesitate. I was down to 750 shares by now, having sold a little each time the stock seesawed above 16. I immediately bought 1,250 more. And three days later came that second-quarter earnings report that earned me eight thousand dollars in a day. Terra Incognita, whoever she was, was making me rich.

Dear Laura:

> Well, I guess it's obvious by now that we seem to be able to live without each other. Do you even remember the last time we spoke in person (i.e. w/o telephone answering machines or e-mail)? I know I've been hard to connect with lately, but shouldn't this lack of contact be telling us something? Well shit, here I am breaking up with you, and I'm doing it via e-mail . . . <DELETE> <DELETE> <DELETE>

Osiris went crazy for the next week. On Thursday, it went up four points; on Friday, another two-and-change. Over the weekend, there was an article in *Barron's* that mentioned Osiris very favorably, and so the stock rallied again on Monday. I was making serious money now, and so were lots of other people. They left ecstatic messages on the board—prozacboy even talked about buying a twin for his beloved orange Boxster—and the "I Love Terra" thread was busier than ever. "This is Nirvana, man," Warren wrote me. "We've all been waiting a long time for this stock to take off. Now it's payback time."

But through it all, Terra herself was silent. She disappeared entirely from the board for days, then weeks. The "I Love Terra" posts started sounding a little desperate. She seemed to be ignoring us. And so we whined:

> terra? terra, are you there? where ARE you, dammit??
> —hawk71

Meanwhile, Laura stopped calling and started writing e-mails:

> Peter:
> Is there something wrong with your answering machine? I'm beginning to think you might be a jerk. Please call or write to disabuse me of this notion. Love,
> Laura

Then came the news:

> URGENT!!! See referenced article from ZDNet. It's about Terra.
> —Phil-R-Up

At the end of his post was a link to a news item. Breathless, I clicked on it, waited for it to display, and then read:

> SEC INVESTIGATES "IRREGULARITIES"
>
> (Washington, June 24) The Securities and Exchange Commission today launched an investigation into allegations of securities vio-

lations and other trading irregularities involving an employee of Osiris Software Inc., an Internet appliance software maker based in Vienna, Virginia.

According to an affidavit filed by the company, Edith Sneed, an assistant to the manager of strategic alliances at Osiris, communicated to friends and former colleagues confidential information about the company's quarterly revenues and pending deal negotiations with potential partner firms. The affidavit also alleges that Ms. Sneed posted similar information pseudonymously on at least one Internet message board devoted to discussions of Osiris stock. . . .

I was up for most of the night. I lay in bed in my clothes, feeling sick, listening to the traffic go by on the street below my window. The name—Edith Sneed—was horrible, like some character from Dickens who abused children or something. But I tried not to let it get in the way. This woman, Edith Sneed, had sacrificed her entire career for the sake of me and a couple dozen other men she'd never met. It didn't matter whether she had benefited herself from the inside information; her leaking it to us was an act of total unselfishness. And I just couldn't understand it.

The next day was an issue-closing at work, so I didn't get home until late. I logged on after dinner, bleary-eyed and exhausted. But I didn't go to the Osiris message board. Instead, I looked up Edith Sneed on 411.com. There were about a dozen listed, but only one anywhere near corporate headquarters in Vienna, Virginia. I printed out the information and called the telephone number listed. There was no answer—not even a machine. I hung up, walked around my apartment a few times, then went back to the computer and grabbed the printout from my desk.

On the drive over to Virginia, I told myself I was an idiot. What was I expecting to happen? I imagined myself driving up to her house—some little suburban ranch, say—and ringing the doorbell. Who would answer? Some sweet, matronly woman with white hair? A goateed, tattooed husband with bad teeth? Or maybe the faceless woman in my dream? "Hi," I'd say, "my name is Peter. I'm the Huddite, and I just wanted to be with you in your time of trouble." And what would she do? Would she laugh at me? Slam the door in my face? Rush into my arms and promise to become mine forever?

The address turned out to be an immaculate little townhouse in a huge development not far from the Metro station in Vienna. Each unit had an identical spotless garbage can in its driveway, strapped to a railing with one of those elastic ropes with hooks on each end. Impatiens and geraniums were arranged along the concrete walks in rows so perfectly straight that you were tempted to kick a few over.

There was no car in the driveway, but I went up to the front door anyway and rang the bell. After a few agonizing seconds, it was clear that I wasn't going to get an answer. "Dickhead," I muttered. I stepped back and checked the second-floor windows, but I knew I was just wasting my time.

"You looking for Edith Sneed?"

I turned. There was a guy in a weird kind of silver jogging suit on the sidewalk behind me. He wore thick glasses and an odd little skullcap, like an Arab, though he seemed more German-looking than anything.

"Is she around?"

"I don't know," he said. "I was looking for her myself."

"You a friend of hers?"

He looked embarrassed. "Sort of. I know her, a little. From the Internet."

"The Osiris message board?" I asked.

I could see from his face that I was right. I held out my hand. "My name's Peter. I'm the Huddite."

"You're kidding me. *The* Huddite? I'm AxelBroder."

We shook hands. I guess I should have felt embarrassed or humiliated to be found out like that, but there wasn't time, since right then another car pulled up. It was an orange Boxster, and out of it popped a scrawny young guy with sneakers, baggy shorts, and a tie-dyed muscle shirt. No question in my mind who this was. "Hey prozacboy," I said.

It turned into a party. Or maybe it turned into a wake. prozacboy had two bottles of tequila in his car, and the three of us sat on Terra's front step, drinking. AxelBroder told us he lived on Capitol Hill and had taken the Metro out, but prozacboy had driven in all the way from Youngstown, Ohio—without stopping. "Hey, man, you see that vehicle over there?" he asked, gesturing at his Boxster. "Two-thirds of that is Terra's doing. I had to come."

We got slowly but determinedly shit-faced. Each of us took turns at the tequila bottle, pausing between slugs to make heartfelt and increasingly maudlin orations on Terra Incognita and the sacrifices she had made for us, the generosity she had shown us, the goddam love she had given us. AxelBroder showed us a little book he'd made on his computer—"The Complete Osiris Postings of Terra Incognita"—and instead of thinking the guy the biggest loser-geek on earth, I sympathized. I even broke down and told them about my dream fragment about her. "The bats," prozacboy intoned when I finished. "The bats mean something important. And the canoe, man—obviously phallic."

By midnight, things began to wind down. AxelBroder said good-night and wandered off toward the Metro; prozacboy fell asleep on the lawn. Feeling comfortably buzzed, I sat down on the grass beside him, finishing the last few ounces of tequila and wondering if it would be dangerous just to leave him there on the lawn, alone. "Hey, prozac," I said, pushing his shoulder. "You should sleep it off in that car of yours. You'll get rheumatism or something on this grass." But he was totally gone. Sighing, I got to my feet, grabbed one of his hands, and tried to pull him up.

And that's when Terra appeared at the end of the walk.

"Excuse me," she said—half cautious question, half annoyed assertion. I turned. It's strange, but I'd been so prepared to be surprised by who she was that I was doubly surprised when she turned out to be exactly like my fantasies of her. Not beautiful, but young and attractive—in her early thirties, long, auburnish hair pulled back tight, a kind of feline softness to her features. She was wearing worn black jeans and a white T-shirt with a little MicroDesign logo on the pocket. "Can I ask what you're doing on my lawn?" She had one hand in her bag, probably grabbing for a can of pepper spray.

"You're Terra, aren't you?" I asked. "Or Edith, I mean? Edith Sneed?"

Her face cloaked a little. "Who are you?"

"I'm the Huddite." I kicked the crumpled pile at my feet. "And this is prozacboy. We came to say thanks."

"Oh my god," she said. She took a step back and put a hand up to her chest like a bad actress expressing surprise in a movie. But then her expression changed. "Jesus, Huddite. I feel like I know you." She was smiling, and I felt that maybe it wasn't so stupid of me to be there. Finally, after some obvious internal process of risk-assessment, she asked me: "You want to come in for tea?"

Together, we grabbed prozacboy by the armpits and lugged him into the house. We dumped him onto the couch in the living room, and then I followed her into the kitchen. Like the rest of the house, it was tidy and nondescript, with a few girly touches—artificial greenery, fussy little window treatments—all of which screamed "recently divorced" as loudly as a sheaf of separation papers would have.

I watched as Terra went through the motions of filling the kettle from the tap, twisting on the gas range, and stuffing tea bags into two green mugs.

"So you're in trouble." This was my brilliant attempt to restart the conversation.

"You might say that. I'll never eat lunch in the New Economy again, that's for sure." Then she crossed her arms and said, "Look, I don't know why you all went and tracked me down like this, but if you're worried about trouble with the SEC or Osiris, you shouldn't. None of you had any idea who I was, so you can't be charged with any trading violations or anything like that. For all you knew, I was just a lucky guesser."

"That's not why I'm here," I said.

"Okay, then. Why *are* you here?"

I shrugged. "Like I said, I wanted to thank you. And I guess I just needed to know why you gave us all that information. When you must have known what could happen if you were caught."

"Oh, geez, I don't know, Hud—or Peter, that's your name, right? I read your profile." This embarrassed her. She looked away. "Why does anybody do anything? I'd been following the board for months before I said boo, and you all seemed so funny and loopy, and so totally clueless about Osiris stock. I just thought I'd help you out."

"But you didn't even know us."

She laughed. "Yeah, I didn't. It's ridiculous, isn't it?"

The water was boiling. She poured some into each mug and carried them over to the kitchen table. "It's been a rough year for me," she said, turning her back toward me as she got some spoons. "I guess I just wanted a little adoration for a change. And god, did you all oblige, especially prozacboy out there." She turned to face me. "Hey, he's kinda cute, isn't he? In a skateboardy kind of way?"

I didn't answer. It's strange, but all I could think about was the fact that Terra was right here before me, that she was perfect, *perfect*—attractive, simpatico, everything. And yet, despite all of that, I had to admit that *she wasn't what I wanted.* My fantasy had landed on a platter in front of me—*thwok!*—but just as it landed, my own wanting had gone somewhere else. I want to be clear: Terra was in no way a disappointment. But all I could feel was this sense of release, of being set free.

"I should go," I said then, a little abruptly.

This seemed to hit her. I saw her eyes cut to the untouched mugs of tea, then cut away to the kitchen window. "Do you have to?" she asked. "I thought you might like to stay."

I couldn't have dreamed it better than this, I told myself. She was propositioning me—I was *sure* she was propositioning me. She had looked up my profile, after all. She'd been as intrigued by me as I had been by her. Before.

"I've got a girlfriend," I blurted after an awkward pause. "She's home right now." This was bad enough, but then I said something *really* lame: "Maybe next time."

She seemed to flinch at this. "Yeah," she said. "Maybe." She carried both cups of tea to the sink and poured them out. When she turned back, she was all business: "But listen, I can't let you drive home after all that tequila or whatever it is you two have been drinking. I'll call you a cab."

She moved past me into the living room to make the call. I watched her go, thinking of my dream, wondering why I wasn't wondering if I was making a mistake. But my itch to leave now was almost unbearable. I felt I had to get home and get *started,* though on what I had no idea.

"They'll be here in two minutes," she said, coming back. "The taxi stand is just over by the Metro, so it doesn't take them long."

"You'll be okay here? I mean, with prozacboy on your couch?"

"He looks harmless enough. Besides, I'm too old for him. Isn't he the one who likes fourteen-year-old girls? Or was that eddiehaskell?"

"No, it was him."

We walked into the living room and stood side by side, looking down at prozacboy. He had a line of drool running down his chin and into the frilly cushions.

"I guess you can wait for the cab outside," she said.

"Okay," I said, feeling awful suddenly. "Good luck with your legal problems. Let me know if there's anything I can do. To help, I mean. And thanks—for being such a good sport."

"That's me, Peter," she said bitterly, "always a good sport." Then, brightening suddenly, she went over to the phone table and wrote something down on a pad. She ripped the page out, folded it, and handed it to me. "Open this when you get into the cab. Whether you do anything about it is your decision. Just make sure you toss this paper and forget I ever gave it to you." She pushed me toward the door. "Now go."

One of those dilapidated Virginia cabs—a rusted yellow Impala—was waiting at the curb. I walked slowly down the walkway toward it, fingering the piece of paper Terra had given me. When I got in, I looked out the window toward the door, but she had already pushed it closed.

The driver, a rail-thin Vietnamese kid who looked barely old enough to drive, looked back at me expectantly.

"Just head to Dupont Circle," I told him. "I'll direct you from there."

As we pulled away from the curb, I unfolded the little note. It read, in small, perfectly formed handwriting:

formal takeover bid from totura sometime in the next 2 weeks. probably $25–30/share. osiris will accept. happy trails. —terra

I folded the paper again and stuffed it into my pocket. This woman was incredible, I told myself. She'd just given me the chance I needed to remake my whole life. Tomorrow, I would put everything I had into Osiris. I'd borrow from my mother, from my brother, and leverage it all on margin. Conceivably, I could make enough to move to L.A. *and* pay for a year or two of grad school.

The cab driver's eyes met mine in the rearview. "You my first fare ever," he said. "I get my cabbie license today, first time."

"Congratulations," I said. "Just promise me you won't crash." Then I leaned back, closed my eyes, and let myself be taken home to bed.

NO YELLERS

Chris Offutt

This whole notion of an electronics singles club is new to me. I will never admit to doing this. Right off the bat, you need to know that I have never placed or answered an ad of this nature. I'm not a businessman seeking discreet afternoon fun, or a New Yorker looking for a fellow snobby Ivy Leaguer, or a rural single hoping to end lonely days (and nights) far from town.

The woman who runs this cyber café explained the Internet until the cows came home. She is patient. The best I can figure is that it's like a magazine on your computer, and you can turn the pages, read what's there, and stick something up for other folks to see.

According to the chart she gave me, I am a SWM NS ND, but what I feel like is a lonely man. I don't seek friendship and maybe more. I want the whole kit and caboodle. Part of me doesn't care who you are or what you look like, but that seems like a bad thing to put here. I do care. I'm very caring. If I didn't care, I wouldn't be imagining that you, a stranger staring at a fake magazine somewhere, would have an interest in me.

Which brings me to the main things—who are you and what do

you want? I hope you're reading this because you're shy, not desperate. I don't think I'm desperate, but I wonder if this is a desperate act—paying twenty-five dollars by credit card to write whatever I want, then have access to what women write.

I am forty-two and it is hard to date at my age, hard to meet women when you live in the country—harder still when you don't like country music, sitting in bars, or going to church. I have a few male friends, but the only women they know are aunts or sisters. When you get right down to it, I don't have all that many male friends, either. Men require some form of activity in order to be together, but I despise sports. I'll be damned before I join a men's group and pound my leather drum and share my greatest macho moment with a bunch of fearful, neurotic, deformed, insecure, overly sensitive misfits who'd complain if you hung them with a new rope. I'd rather be alone.

Still, I want to live with you. Yes, you. I don't like going to bed alone, and the mornings are even worse. On the weekends, I will sometimes go to a store just to hear someone speak. Do you ever get lonesome for a voice? I don't mean lonely, which has always seemed to be an inner state, possibly even normal, but I'm talking about flat-out lonesome for another living being in the house, not counting plants and animals. I don't understand people who have pets instead of friends, but don't get me wrong—animal lovers are welcome in my life.

This whole electronic deal makes me as nervous as a long-tailed cat in a room full of rocking chairs. I'm afraid my neighbors will somehow learn it was me who wrote this. I'm afraid of coming off utterly pathetic, like a wacked-out loner, or a psycho rural type. One thing I should mention is that I am not a gun owner. I'm not against them, but I don't see the need to have one. It's easier to buy meat at the grocery store than to hunt. I don't own a pickup truck either. I don't smoke or do drugs. I will upon occasion drink wine, but only at night and never alone—which means I've been sober lately. I'm not a fanatic gym guy with muscles so swelled that my head seems small by comparison, but I do walk a mile a day. I have a steady income and a certain amount of savings. I'm not the handsomest man who ever came down the pike, but not the ugliest either.

It is easier to tell you what I am not, rather than what I am. Maybe this is why I don't know what kind of woman I want. I'm open-minded. What's best for me is to describe what I don't want, so if the shoe fits, you can nix yourself right out of the mix.

Say for example your back has been out for three weeks. You refuse to take care of it—or take care of yourself. I have been doing the cooking, the cleaning, and the laundry. I get medicine for you, arrange appointments with chiropractors and massage therapists. I don't mind doing this. I enjoy it, in fact. Taking care of you is part of loving you. I enjoy being someone you can depend on.

Are you Internet women with me so far? Because I'm going to go on a little bit. I'm not some nut who needs to be needed, and will only be happy with an incontinent woman in a wheelchair with her hair falling out and her fingers rotting off. That's not what I want. I want someone who doesn't mind being loved on a little bit.

Let's say I know your back hurts like a migraine. You don't sleep well. You can barely walk, and when you do, your posture is crooked as a dog's hind leg. Getting in and out of the car is hard, and backing up is nearly impossible because you can't quite turn your head to see safely behind you. I will drive you if you ask, but you don't ask for anything. After three weeks that started getting to me.

When you run out of overnight back medicine with a sleep inducer, you don't replace it. You don't see a doctor or exercise. You don't pour hot baths and sprinkle in the special powder I got in town. You don't accept help from your women friends. You don't rest. You won't admit that your body is off its feed.

When I brought this up, you got mad as a wet hornet. It was like your marrow turned molten and was burning inside each bone. You turned red-faced and began yelling. Strands of drool hung between your lips, and drops went flying out of your mouth. Your ankles and hands twitched like you were on trucker pills. You aged right in front of me as if from the inside out, your lovely face pulling into deep furrows. Dark hammocks appeared beneath each eye socket.

All this happened while you were screaming your head off at me. I treated you like a queen and you acted like I was filling your royal goblet with poison.

You became furious that I stayed calm. You said I was mad at you for being sick. You said I resented taking care of you.

I said that's not true. I said you were mad at yourself for being sick. I said you were mad at me for saying you needed to take better care of yourself.

Whew, doggies, that last part sparked you up big time. I thought steam was going to rise off your head. You yelled and yelled and I had to look at your ear, which is beautiful by the way, because I couldn't bear seeing any more flying saliva. I kept telling myself it wasn't personal, that your back hurt like an impacted wisdom tooth. After two hours, I left for work and when I returned, you erupted again and continued until after midnight. You wore me out but I could not sleep. The worst of it was you pushed me away then accused me of being distant.

I have to stop and say that if any of this holds any truth for any of you women reading this, do me a favor and just skip to the next name on the list. Please leave me alone. I've had my turn with you. My dad yelled at me the whole time I was a kid and I admit I am sensitive to it. I understand that some couples blow off steam by fighting, then make up with sex. Those people need to find each other. I'm just not built that way. I am not a hippie but I like peace and love.

You accuse me of being contemptuous and scornful and selfish. It is never my actual words you get upset with, but how you interpret my tone, which leaves me without any level ground. I can't contradict you because you are quick to claim that your interpretation is valid. Somebody's feelings are always real. You cannot judge feelings. Invariably you say something mean over your shoulder as you are walking out of the room, then go lie on your side of the bed and wait for me to come and make you feel better. Sometimes I'm just not up to the chore. If I don't take you in my arms and forgive you on the spot, you get mad and we're back to spit city again.

Pretty soon you're back to red-faced yelling with that saliva acting like it's got a life of its own. Finally you exhaust yourself. You approach me but stop at arm's length, and say in a monotone, "I love you. I'm sorry." Often you will say it again in the same dull, flat voice. It's not an apology or a declaration of love. The only time you say you love me is when you feel bad for mistreating me.

Anyhow, you got up from bed while I was making you lunch. You sat at the table. You didn't come into the kitchen to say hi, or give me a hug or a kiss. You sat and waited for food. Your posture was excellent because of your back, perhaps the only good thing to come of your malady. Your hair had golden highlights from the morning sun that washed in the window. I'd just completed vacuuming the dining room and living room because I know it hurts your back to run the sweeper. I was making you soup and a sandwich. You sat at the drop-leaf maple table I gave you a month ago and began to yell at me.

You said all my effort made you feel beholden to me, and you resented feeling vulnerable. You called me a few names. Your face was red and the spit was on your chin. I served your lunch. You gobbled it up and didn't say thanks.

The saddest part is that none of this upset me. I've become numb, plus I know it's because your back hurts like a dog bite. What made me mad came later. You were willing to let me leave for work without making any effort to smooth things out. I pointed this out and you followed me to the door. I thought maybe you'd give me a kiss, but you said you couldn't talk to me because my anger made you uncomfortable.

I drove to work with those words ringing in my head. I wanted to write them down so I wouldn't forget them, but there was no need—I'll remember them a long time. You can yell at me but I'm not supposed to respond because it might make you uncomfortable. Halfway to work, I called in sick, and kept on going. I just boogied on down the road. That was six months ago.

So if any of this sounds like the kind of woman you are, you can just mouse-click me out of your life. I am fed up with your type. I don't want love, I want a friend.

I rented a small place on the edge of the nearest college town. Young kids live all around me. They are a dazzling bunch, their skin covered with pictures and their faces full of metal. The other day in a diner, I saw a girl remove a stud from the space below her lower lip and squirt milk from the hole. I have to admit, it tickled me no end.

I've tried to tell you what I'm not, but what I am is anybody's guess. I know some of you might think only a big jerk would leave a woman with a bad back, but I did my best. Besides, I called her and she was better. She said as soon as I went out, her back went in. So it was all my fault after all.

I have to admit I feel like a moron in this cyber café. I am the oldest person by fifteen years, and no one looks at me like I'm a cool older guy. Beside me are two guys with ragged goatees playing a video game with two shaved-head guys across the room. They are laughing and having fun, and I can't remember when I did either. I have entered a new world. Living here makes me feel young, and I have been thinking of getting a tattoo. It will say "No Yellers." I will casually roll my sleeves up when I am around women who interest me.

A man is never too old to change, I say. I'm not running off to the piercing parlor, but I know how to monkey around with the Internet. I kind of like having a secret username. I don't know how to get these words onto the magazine page for you to see. I'll ask the woman who runs this place. She has so much metal hanging off her face, it would be like kissing a tackle box, but I like her anyhow. She's nice to me. She said she's rooting for me to find you. She said you're out there. She said I was a good catch.

So I'll check back tomorrow. I promise to write to all and sundry.

MINESWEEPER

David Liss

To Warren's mind, Sandra Quint carried a good twenty pounds more than she ought to have if she were looking to appeal to the average guy—who did she think she was kidding with those big arms?—but Warren, who had his own body issues, was not the average guy. He found himself drawn to women who weighed a little extra—not necessarily because he found them attractive, but because he convinced himself that he would have better luck with women who might be self-conscious about their looks. While a perfectly sound idea, it had so far failed to yield much in the way of results.

Other than being a bit on the chunky side, Sandra Quint was distractingly pretty. She had a perfect heart-shaped face, piercing blue eyes, and black-rooted bleached hair pulled back in a short ponytail. She liked to display her enormous breasts in low-cut tank tops.

He had seen her around the department for the past few months, but hadn't found a chance to talk to her before now, so this, he knew, was his big chance.

"I guess you like Henry James," he said, his eyes pointed somewhere between her breasts and her face.

"I just need the course distribution requirements form," she explained. She looked at her Swatch.

"You know," he pressed. "Peter Quint from 'The Turn of the Screw.' "

"That's interesting," said Sandra Quint, who was a medievalist and very possibly did not know Henry James from a hole in her ass. She had a dry, surprisingly deep voice. Warren liked women with high, squeaky voices, since they were invariably nicer to him. Still, he liked Sandra's voice too.

"I don't really like to read Henry James, but there have been a bunch of movies; all of them kind of suck, but the Lynn Redgrave one is probably best. Then there's *The Nightcomers,* with Marlon Brando—I guess a prehistory of Quint. You're not likely to come across it by accident, but if you like obscure Marlon Brando movies, it's worth looking for. If you're stupid enough to go to those shitty chain video places, you won't find it. But Lost Reel on Federal Highway has it."

"Hey, that's interesting," the uninterested Sandra Quint told him as she grabbed her course distribution requirements sheet and fled.

Warren paused for a moment before looking up to see if Edgardo had witnessed the exchange, but Edgardo typed away furiously, trying to get the department chair's letters perfect before the big meeting with the provost. That idiot had been working in the department for six months, and he still killed himself trying to get every little thing done.

Warren took a moment to decide whether he wanted to lean back to look at the clock on the wall or play a game of Minesweeper on the computer. The clock won: it said 11:30. "I'm going to lunch," he announced.

"Have fun," Edgardo answered wearily, while Warren walked toward the kitchen area. Edgardo knew perfectly well that no one would see Warren again before 1:30 or 2:00.

The office's little kitchen area smelled of burned coffee, spoiled cheese, and regular, nondescript garbage. Warren held his breath, as if he were diving into a pool, before heading into the tiny room to retrieve his bagged lunch from the departmental fridge. He always stuck his stuff in the back, lodging it behind the two containers of key lime yogurt he'd bought and partially opened last year. No one would go near the food back there in the refrigerator's fuzziest section. Tucker, the department chair, kept getting on his case about cleaning out the refrigerator. But Jesus Christ—was he the maid?

Once in the hallway outside the English department, Warren took a moment to figure out where it would be best to pass his lunch break. Braver Hall, in which the English department resided on the sixth floor, was the oldest of the South Florida State buildings. It had that industrial look about it, with narrow hallways carpeted in the most institutional beige yet invented, cork bulletin boards announcing student productions of Shakespeare, and broken desks and chairs that had been piled outside classrooms, awaiting some bureaucratic procedure that would banish them to a mysterious basement. Still, it was better than Krieger Hall, Warren's least-favorite building on campus, which was a converted parking garage where every floor slanted at a twenty-five-degree angle.

In the hallway, near grad-student mail cubbyholes, Warren saw Sandra Quint talking with a couple of other students whose names he could not be bothered to summon. He knew them from around the office, and they had repeatedly pissed Warren off by just being their cocky selves. What the hell kind of grad student worked out and wore tight T-shirts showing off muscles like some kind of moron? They ought to be too busy with their reading to find time to pump iron like a bunch of idiots.

Warren walked over to Sandra, who was listening to one of the other students talk about some article he had sent off to a major journal.

"I still think *Excalibur* is the best King Arthur movie out there," Warren said to Sandra while one of her friends was in midsentence, "even if it is a little weird. But you're a medievalist and all. You probably like it."

All three of them stared. Warren had long ago learned that if he simply started a conversation with someone, even if that person had been talking to someone else, he could usually take control of things. The trick was to keep eye contact, act as if the others were simply not there. Most people would be too surprised to resist him.

It worked reasonably well in this case. Sandra's two companions clammed up. She said, her voice strangely quiet, "I've never seen it." She looked at her friends and then the floor.

"You've never seen it? I really think you ought to. I think you ought to see it tonight."

Having said his piece, and not wanting to talk to the weight lifters, Warren pushed on, moving past the elevator bank and around the corner to the hallway with the professors' offices. There, under the fluorescent lights, he pressed his memory into service to recall the day of the week. Wednesday. Of course. Rick never came in on Wednesdays. Warren walked to the end of the hall, last door on the right, and opened it with his departmental passkey. He knew who came in and who didn't on what days, when they had classes and when they had meetings. On any given day he found the best office to hole up in, and he could get in and out without anyone ever knowing he'd been there. As long as he cleaned up after lunch it would all be fine.

Warren especially liked using Rick's office. Rick had brought in a comfortable couch perfect for napping, though who knew what else Rick might use it for. He was just the sort to slip one in with wide-eyed and unsuspecting undergraduates. He probably liked girls in tight tank tops, like Sandra Quint wore.

Warren set down his lunch bag and began to peek at the correspondence lying on Rick's desk. He knew what all the professors were up to, and he knew Rick's business best of all—what journals had rejected his articles, what conferences he planned to attend. Warren particularly enjoyed going through Rick's things, taking his paper clips and rubber bands, leafing through his books, examining the quality of the spare shirts and underwear he kept tucked away, checking out the copies of *Men's Health* and *Maxim* he hid behind the filing cabinet. Rick was a fucking asshole.

He took a moment to fantasize about Sandra Quint, wearing nothing but panties and a camisole, watching one of the movies he had suggested to her. Then he logged on to Rick's computer—the idiot used his birthday for a password and therefore deserved to have his system hacked—and went to his personals account. One message from Kimmy in South Dakota wondering why her last three e-mails had gone unanswered. The reason, Warren thought, is because you're repulsive. Did she really think that pic she'd sent would keep the letters coming? Maybe the men she knew in South Dakota liked bony women with gaunt, haggard faces, overbleached hair, and stupidly tight jeans, but Warren knew white trash when he saw it. The comparisons Kimmy had made between herself and Faith Hill had failed to come through. Of course Warren, or Jake, as he called himself in his ads, had told Kimmy that he liked country girls just fine, but he lived in Florida—he didn't need to send e-mails halfway across the world for this trailer-park bullshit. Warren thought back to all the messages he'd traded with Kimmy—the misspellings, the grammatical errors, the stupid opinions, the love of romance novels. He should have noticed these things, but until you see the pic, you can always hope for the best.

But better material lay ahead. Jake had received a message from Heather, who Warren had no doubt would remain in his favor for some time. She had sent a couple of photos in her latest message, and she looked just as she had described herself: pale skin, blue eyes, and medium-length dark hair. In one of the pics she wore a tight and low-cut T-shirt that showed off a medium-sized but nicely proportioned pair. In the other pic she sat at her desk in her office, and pictures of all the living presidents hung on the wall behind her. Heather worked as the secretary for a vice president at a rental car company located outside Milwaukee. He found that drearily delicious. The ones with boring jobs in boring places always got hooked. Warren didn't want anything to do with anyone New York or L.A. or San Francisco. Wyoming and Idaho produced the women who lasted longest.

Heather's letter turned out to be provocative and teasing without being explicitly sexy. Warren liked that. Some of the women he'd written to liked to talk dirty almost right away: tell me your favorite position, what is the strangest place you ever did it. Not for Warren, thank you. Maybe later on, when things got serious, but if the sex surfaced too quickly, Warren grew suspicious: psycho, or more likely, man in disguise. Anyone who sent a nude pic right away was also almost certainly a male asshole loser who couldn't face up to being gay. Warren had nothing against gays; sometimes his ads, which were so perfectly constructed they should have won him a Nobel prize, attracted some hopeful gay interest. These queries— Warren liked the pun—always met with polite replies: thank you very much for your flattering interest, I'm only looking to meet women, but best of luck to you. Warren believed in being polite.

So that he could script his reply perfectly, Warren read Heather's letters a couple of times. It was important to match someone's intelligence, sense of humor, interests, and general disposition if you were going to form some kind of bond. It took him about forty-five minutes to get his four-paragraph reply in perfect order. He showed some wit, threw out a couple of casual details that made him interesting, demonstrated sympathy for Heather's horrible marriage, and signed off with cheerful expectation. And, of course, he would have to attach a couple of photos.

Warren glanced up to the corkboard where Asshole Rick had tacked a dozen photos of himself: Rick on the beach, showing off his tan and muscles; Rick in a suit at a friend's wedding; Rick in sport coat giving a paper on Eliza Haywood at an eighteenth-century lit conference; Rick sitting at a bar with friends, looking just tipsy enough to show the world that, despite academic success, he knew how to have a good time. The guy thought he was a model or something. It had been no problem to steal the pictures, scan then, and put them back all in the space of an hour. Rick never knew that Warren was spreading his image to lonely housewives and hopeful spinsters in the far-flung corners of these United States.

———

Warren was thirty-eight years old, and not nearly as unattractive as he had led himself to believe, but sometime in his early twenties he had settled into the role of the ugly man, and he found a certain dependable comfort there. He was a bit on the short side, and he had allowed himself to round out over the years, but he had rounded out proportionately, distributing his fat with meticulous evenhandedness, so he appeared more soft than heavy. If he had been able to examine his life with anything like clarity, he would have recognized that by now, and indeed since at least the sixth grade, he had no greater enemy than his own personal style. He wore his hair longish, in a Meet-the-Beatles shag, and he had bushy muttonchop sideburns that reminded people in the department of a distracted barrister on the cover of a paperback Dickens novel; he knew that some of the graduate students had taken to calling him Mr. Havisham behind his back, and they called the English department the Circumlocution Office.

And then there were his clothes. Warren had met Anne, his college girlfriend, while wearing a vintage olive blazer and green jeans. Things had not lasted more than a semester with Anne, but Warren now owned two dozen blazers, in various shades of green, and four pairs of green Levi's. Thanks in part to his sideburns, on those occasions that he chose to wear his green fedora he looked impossibly like a leprechaun.

Warren returned to his desk at a quarter after one, green blazer unbuttoned, exposing a tuxedo shirt underneath. He'd barely sat down when Tucker popped his head out of his office. "Can I see you in here a minute, Warr?" Only Tucker called him Warr.

The chair's office, in the corner of the main English department office, looked like the site of a DEA search. Documents lay sprawled out over every possible surface. Books were piled, rather than stacked, haphazardly on the floor. Even the pictures on the wall hung crooked. Mort Tucker was, by all estimates, the worst department chair in the university. He had won the job in part because no one else had wanted it and in part because no one had not wanted Tucker to have it, but his policy of delay and obfuscation had turned him into the most hated person on the faculty. Hires had fallen through because Tucker had failed to make the necessary follow-up calls. Junior professors had been denied tenure because Tucker hadn't remembered to send files to the administrative offices. But Tucker was due not only to step down at the end of the next year, but to retire as well, and so even his most vicious enemies thought it best simply to wait him out.

"Listen, Warr. Have a seat," he said. He remained behind his desk, fanning himself with a thick folder despite the fact that the office was over-air-conditioned. Tucker had come from Canada, and even looking out his window at the south Florida landscape made him sweat.

Warren had a seat and waited for it.

"Warr, we've had some complaints." Tucker had a thin face, and he had a habit of sucking in his cheeks during pauses in conversation. "A couple of the graduate students, and I'm not going to name names, have come to me and told me that you've been just a little, well, rude to them. That you don't like to hand over the documents they need, you give them a hard time when they hand things over to you. That you make them wait unnecessarily."

"Other graduate students," Warren said.

"What?"

"I'm also a graduate student, so the complaints have come from 'other graduate students' not 'graduate students.' "

"Of course. The thing is, we've talked about this before. Dealing with other graduate students is part of your job, and it just isn't right to make them feel like they're wasting your time when they have questions or need something."

"I'm not sure," Warren muttered.

"You know, we've been awfully lenient here with you. You take long lunches, you take a lot of sick days, and no one gives you a hard time about it. You've been working in the department for quite a while now, and you're an important part of the team, but in certain areas you just haven't been holding up your end."

"I think we ought to rearrange the office," Warren replied. "It would be better to move the desks so they face the door rather than keeping them perpendicular to the door."

"That seems like a good idea," Tucker said slowly, and then proceeded to talk with Warren for fifteen minutes on the virtues of rearranging the desks. Finally, when the desk conversation appeared to have run its course, Tucker tried to regroup. "These complaints I mentioned before. I think they're worth talking about."

"Sometimes," Warren said under his breath, not entirely aware that his response had nothing to do with Tucker's statement.

"I hope you will at least think about what I've said."

Warren sighed and then did his best to telegraph boredom. He leaned back in his chair, crossed his legs, and examined his nails, which he trimmed to almost painful shortness every other day.

Tucker did not dare fire him. Tucker did not dare make things difficult for him. Though he might be lazy, he got the things done he had to, including the things no one else could do. Good luck finding the files for the new hire. What chance would they have in locating the tenure-review forms? There were dozens of documents, dozens of procedures, that Warren had buried over the years in byzantine filing systems and within inscrutable layers of computer file trees. If Warren left, it would take the department a year to get back up to speed.

"I've had some stuff going on," he finally offered, knowing that he needed to offer something, but really his thoughts hovered around Heather and some clever lines he wished he had included in his e-mail. He might send her another one right after work, even if she had not yet replied to the first. He already had her hooked, and he couldn't think of a good reason not to show her his interest.

"Anything you care to talk about?"

"No," Warren said. "It's okay now."

"Good," Tucker said. "That's just the way I like it."

———

It had been eleven years since Warren had enrolled in the doctoral program at South Florida State, located thirty miles west of Fort Lauderdale. It was, depending on who you talked to, either a low second-tier school or a high third-tier one. South Florida had been the only program to offer Warren any kind of fellowship package, so he hadn't been in a position to say no. Nevertheless, he had hated to leave New York, where he had grown up and gone to college. His B.A. from Columbia had not been the result of especially impressive grades, but Warren had managed to steal enough English department stationery to forge a few wonderfully crafted letters of recommendation. They hadn't quite done the trick at Harvard or Berkeley, but they'd been good enough to get by the admissions committee at South Florida State.

Warren hated Florida, with its ubiquitous SUVs and strip malls and vacuous women in shorts. He hated living in a place where failure to use air-conditioning could be fatal. He hated the Hooters and the Houlihans and the ChiChis that littered the landscape. No one had stared at him in New York, but they stared here—in shopping malls, in grocery stores, on line waiting to rent videos.

Still, with his grades he'd been happy to get into South Florida State at the time, and he'd begun the doctoral program with a great deal of energy, envisioning a dissertation that would rethink the eighteenth-century origins of the novel—despite his advisers warning him that "origin of the novel" projects were passé. Five years later, with his fellowship expired, and his first chapter outlined sketchily at best, Warren had taken the job in the English department to pay his bills while he finished his work. But the work somehow never got done. He could not even remember the last time he'd looked at his notes.

Meanwhile, along came Rick, who started grad school *after* Warren and had already finished his degree program—at a school not much better than South Florida State, a fact that especially infuriated Warren—and landed a tenure-track job. He'd published about a half-dozen articles in major journals, he and some grad-school buddy of his had edited an essay collection, and his first book, which would allegedly recast the idea of gender in the first half of the eighteenth century, would be published by Cambridge next month. Once it was out, everyone seemed to agree, Rick would be able to wave bye-bye to South Florida State and take some cushy senior-professor job. Warren was just the guy who worked in the English department, but Rick was a hot property.

The next day Rick hovered over Warren's desk. "Were you using my office yesterday?"

Warren tried not to look up. He'd been playing Minesweeper, and he might have been on the verge of an all-time best score. "Office?" he asked. "No, Rick. Why would I?"

"I don't know why you would," he said, "but I found crumbs all over my chair."

He'd forgotten to wipe that down. "I don't know what to tell you. Maybe they were from Tuesday." Warren clicked on the wrong square and set off a mine, so the game was shot to hell. He knew that Minesweeper was a stupid little game—it came preloaded on the computer—but it had a certain appeal. You had to figure out where the mines were without setting any of them off—part logic, part intuition, part thinking fast. It was like working in the English department. It was like meeting women on the Internet. Sometimes when he played he liked to imagine that he had been captured by hostile aliens who made him play for his life. He had to beat a certain score or they would push him out the airlock.

"I didn't eat in my office on Tuesday," Rick said, making no effort to keep his voice down. "Come on, Warren, I've talked to you about this. I don't want you going into my office when I'm not there."

Warren looked up for the first time. Asshole Rick had some sort of expensive shirt, and he wore those tailored pants that made him look like he had no ass. He'd just had his blond, beach-boy hair cut, so he looked unnaturally well groomed. Did women really fall for that blond hair, blue-eyed, tanned thing?

"You've talked to me about it," Warren said. "I didn't go in."

"Goddamn it." Rick allowed a little spittle to fly from his mouth. "You know what the issues are. I don't want anyone in my office. It's not a joke." He dropped a disk on the desk. "I need the document on there printed in the next hour." He walked off.

That was exactly the sort of behavior that left Warren feeling more than justified in his little campaign.

As it turned out, Rick had good reason for his concerns about security in his office. He had a stalker. He had been receiving threatening notes, first by e-mail, and then with scary little packages sent to the department. And he deserved all of it. Every last bit.

This is what happened: Warren had been coasting the men-seeking-women personal ads; he liked to see what tricks the competition might have devised so he might fine-tune his own personality profile. While trawling for ideas he came across an ad for a twenty-nine-year-old professor of English literature living in South Florida. Just how many people out there had a doctorate and a job by the time they were twenty-nine? How many universities were there in South Florida? It had to be Rick. Warren had been pretty sure, but just to be absolutely certain, he'd cobbled together a false female persona and written back, asking for some details: which university, what area he specialized in (his faux female respondent had been an English major in college), and so forth. Just to keep things interesting, Warren threw in the pics from one of the better-looking women with whom he'd hooked up online.

Sure enough, Rick wrote back. They had a hot little correspondence for a while. Rick loved sexual innuendoes. He believed thoroughly in his own cleverness. He boasted that he had no trouble meeting women, but there were so few intelligent people out there. Warren made sure this woman, called Tina, showed herself to be intelligent and funny. She had read a lot, and still loved to read. She had a real interest in eighteenth-century lit, Rick's own area. What were the chances, after all, of Rick meeting another woman who loved to read Pope and Swift?

They traded e-mails, sometimes several each day, and discussed the most intimate things. Tina told Rick how she liked to be kissed, and then, a little later on, how much she enjoyed oral sex. Rick told her that he had always been praised for his great stamina. It was more common than not, he said, for women he was with to have multiple orgasms. Rick wrote that he loved women with big, bushy pubic hair. Rick had the Greek letters of his fraternity tattooed on his ass.

Around the office, Rick walked with an extra spring in his step. He seemed especially cheerful, even to Warren. "I think he's in love," Edgardo speculated. But Warren knew that there was something missing: Rick had not yet met this woman of his dreams. Tina sent him e-mails saying that she had been masturbating while thinking about him, but, inexplicably, she had been unable to find a free evening in her schedule. She had to go out of town for a meeting. Her best friend broke her leg. Rick grew insistent; he wrote that he couldn't help but feel she was putting him off. He wanted to meet her, if only for five minutes, so he could see her in the flesh. At least she could give him his number so they could talk on the phone. Warren could not see a way out, but he hated the idea of ending their exchange. He therefore came up with the most incredible idea: Tina would go psycho.

"You are a fucking asshole," she wrote in her next letter, sent not to his personals mailbox, but to his university e-mail address. (Warren always sent these sorts of things from a free e-mail service that he logged on to from an internet café. No point risking arrest.) "You think you are so fucking smug. How smug are you going to be when we meet for real?"

Rick wrote back. He wanted to know what was going on. He begged her to tell him if he had in some way offended her. Surely there had been some kind of misunderstanding that might be worked out. But Tina just would not engage. Instead, she sent Rick letters in which she flaunted her knowledge of the details of his life. She knew his last name, even though he had never given it to her, his home address, what kind of car he drove. Tina read Rick's published articles and tore them apart for their obviousness and reliance on clever wording rather than original thinking. She began sending notes to Rick in the English department, and then packages that left Rick worrying about bombs. These letters didn't come particularly often. Sometimes more than a month would go by now—enough time to let Rick think she had lost interest. But just when he began to get comfortable, Tina would strike once more.

—

Warren lived in a one-bedroom apartment about five miles from campus on the second floor of a two-story rental complex. He'd once heard that the whole place had been overrun by crack addicts until it had been taken over in the mid-nineties. Now most of the other tenants were transient types—men with long greasy hair tied into ponytails who drove pickup trucks with Confederate flags on the back window, or women with permed hair, too much makeup, and too many screaming kids who always had to be dragged by the arm. The walls of his apartment were paper thin, and he knew when his neighbors sneezed or fucked or thought something was funny.

The apartment did have some advantages besides price. Across the street stood a much more expensive building, ten stories high, and some of the women on the upper floors liked to get undressed without lowering their blinds. Warren kept a pair of high-powered binoculars by the window.

He also improved things by keeping the apartment meticulously tidy. He had six different filing cabinets to help keep all his stuff neat; for example, he had filed every ATM receipt he'd ever received in chronological order going back more than fifteen years. He did not own many books, since he had a library card, which made ownership redundant. But he had ten bookcases of videotapes. *Cops* was the only show he watched with any regularity, and he kept every episode ever aired. He recorded almost everything that he could from American Movie Classics, but he'd seen only about a quarter of the tapes he had in his apartment. He used to try to watch eight or ten movies each weekend, but that was before he got into meeting women online.

A week after Warren had traded pics with Heather, the secretary in Milwaukee, he began to feel that she might be a little something more than most of the women with whom he, in the guise of Jake, had corresponded. Her letters revealed a woman smart, funny, literary, and surprisingly ambitious. In her spare time she was working on a novel (about the Boxer Rebellion—how's that for being not stupid!). She wrote with flair, and her letters often left Warren laughing aloud. Sure, she made some grammatical mistakes, but she made a whole lot fewer than most of the women with whom he'd traded e-mail.

And she did not hide her fascination with Jake.

Over the months, Warren had sculpted the Jake bio until he felt it was smooth enough to be seductive and imperfect enough to be believed. Jake was thirty-three years old. He had worked successfully for a number of years in an advertising firm, but then had dropped out to enroll in the NYU film school. He lived in a big, but not huge, loft in SoHo, which he had inherited from an uncle, of whom he had been very fond and who had died of AIDS five years earlier. Jake was now in the preproduction stages of his thesis film. Meanwhile, a couple of screenplays he'd written were being shopped around Hollywood, and his agent had told him that Ang Lee had shown serious interest in one of them.

Heather took the bait a little too eagerly for Warren's taste. He had hoped for a couple of months of heated e-mail, but she wanted more almost right away. "I wish I could afford to come visit you in New York," Heather wrote. "But I would love to talk to you on the phone. Please give me your number. I want to give you mine, but I don't want to risk my husband finding out about you. I really would love to hear your voice."

Now he found himself with his back against the wall. At this stage, and it had happened many times before, Warren usually stopped responding. The game could advance no further, for he could hardly claim not to have a phone. But Warren didn't want to drop Heather. He liked Heather. He respected her, and he could hardly say that about most of the women to whom he wrote. He found himself thinking about her almost constantly, writing and rewriting letters to her in his head. At times he almost forgot that he was not Jake, or he would fantasize that he might somehow wake up and find himself transformed into Jake, aspiring filmmaker. He would fly out to Wisconsin and rescue Heather from her husband. He would discover that her body was more like Sandra Quint's than he had realized. They would have sex in Jake's hotel room. Jake, who had often been praised for his stamina, would make certain she had multiple orgasms.

And now Heather wanted to talk on the phone, which meant the end of everything—at least, it might have had Warren not possessed the gift of genius. After an agonized half-hour of contemplation, the answer came to him—not at once, but in methodical pieces—and he drove over to Circuit City, where he bought an inexpensive cell phone. When he returned home, he called the provider and gave a false New York City address. The next day, he planned quite cleverly, he would call the phone-service provider back and explain that he'd decided it would be more convenient to have the bill sent to his Florida address. And there he would be, living in Florida but possessing a New York City phone number, and ready to have a real relationship with Heather.

"One question," he said to the customer-service fellow. "Is there any kind of cell phone directory in which my number will be listed?"

"No, sir. These numbers are automatically unlisted."

"What if someone has caller ID or uses *69?"

The man on the other end of the line hesitated for a moment.

"I'm a lawyer," Warren explained, "and it can present problems of client confidentiality if the number isn't blocked."

"I see. The number is blocked automatically. Nothing to worry about, counselor."

So, within four hours of receiving Heather's request for a phone number, Warren had been able to send her one. He loved technology.

Later that evening, the phone, still plugged in to charge the batteries, began to emit its shrill ring to the tune of "Stars and Stripes Forever."

Warren answered after a brief pause and said, "Theo, what's the word?"

On the other end he heard a pretty and crisp female voice. "Oh, I'm sorry. Is this Jake?"

"Yes, it is." His heart beat so hard in his chest for a moment that

Warren feared he might really be having a heart attack. Hot pains shot up his left arm, but they quickly subsided.

"Hi, it's Heather."

"Heather!" he said. "Wow, this is so great. I'm sorry, I was expecting a call from my agent." He opened the "Jake Bio" file on his computer and quickly wrote down that his agent's name was Theo.

"Is this a bad time? Should I call you back?"

"No, it's fine. I have call waiting, and Theo lives on a California schedule. If he says he'll call back tonight, he might call back next week."

She laughed, smooth and delicious. "It's so great to talk to you. You sound just like your picture."

"So do you," he said. "Your voice is very pretty."

She laughed again. "You're such a charmer," she purred.

Conversations like that, he later thought, made him think about taking out a real ad for his real self. What the hell? Maybe he would. Maybe tomorrow. Or the next day.

—

Things continued to build momentum with Heather. They talked every day, sometimes for hours. Warren would bring his cell phone to work and call her during his lunch break. Once he forgot the phone, and called her from the English office anyhow, terrified that this would be the one time she decided to hit *69, but during their next conversation she seemed natural and relaxed, and Warren knew that he had her hooked.

The next week, Warren had been walking down the hall when his cell phone rang. He normally would have let Heather leave a message rather than speak in public, but Sandra Quint had been standing right there. He answered and said, "Hey, sweetheart. I was hoping you'd call." Sandra looked at him, Warren firmly believed, just a little differently after that.

But Heather was the woman he cared about. He hardly ever thought about Sandra anymore. He had stopped sitting in his car outside her apartment, he'd stopped taking out her file and looking over her grades and her course work, and he'd stopped spending hours in the supermarket near her apartment in the hope of running into her.

Who needed Sandra Quint, aloof and self-impressed, when there was Heather? He could talk to her about anything—Jake's film thesis, the morass of Hollywood in which his scripts were lost, his dreams for the future. She talked about her problems with her husband and how grateful she was that they had never had children. Vince, the husband, was a devout Catholic who said that he would never even consider divorce. He also suffered, she said, from terrible depression. He came home from his accounting job, ate, watched TV, and went to bed. He refused to talk about anything except the most unavoidable household concerns: a leaky roof or a broken hot-water heater. They had not had sex in over two years. Once Heather had gone out of town for a long weekend to visit her sister in St. Louis, and Vince had refused to feed the three cats the entire time. He claimed to have forgotten, but when she returned Heather had been able to hear their crying from outside the house.

"For a long time," she explained, "I thought it would be wrong to leave someone who is obviously sick, but he's refused to get help, and now I just don't see that I have any choice. Right now I'm just working up the courage to move out."

Warren would respond with encouraging platitudes that he felt landed flat, but she told him she found his advice extraordinarily helpful. She admired his calm, his ability to think things through. Heather needed someone intelligent and creative and driven— someone like Jake. Talking to him made her think about all the things she wished she could change in her life.

One time she asked Warren to tell her his birthday because she found astrology interesting even if she wasn't sure she believed in it. Warren had made the mistake of answering truthfully, so two weeks later she asked for his address so that she could send him a birthday card.

"Save yourself a stamp," he had told her nervously. "Just send an e-card."

"Oh, I love sending real cards," she'd almost whined. "Some of them are very funny. Do you like 'The Far Side'?"

"I have to tell you something," Warren replied. He could feel his brilliance rising to the surface, bubbling, slick as oil. "The thing is, I'm very active in environmental causes, and I can't condone the use of paper products when they're not necessary. I believe a paperless society is a realistic and necessary goal. I know that a card seems like a little thing, but big things are made of little things. It's very sweet of you to want to send me something, but I just wouldn't feel right."

Heather had been angry and she'd hung up shortly thereafter, but during their next conversation she told him that she found his concern for the environment sexy. If they ever met, she would wear recycled underwear for him.

Then disaster struck. She called him on a Friday afternoon when he was in the middle of a long lunch in an Americanist's office.

"I'm so glad I caught you," she said. Her voice was nearly two octaves higher than usual, and if there had been more than one person who called Warren on the phone, he might not have known who it was. "I have such great news."

He spat out a mouthful of egg salad so he wouldn't sound utterly repulsive. "Great."

"I'm leaving Vince. No, forget that. I've left him! I'm gone. Even as we speak, I'm with my sister in St. Louis. I have a lawyer and everything. I didn't want to tell you about it until it was done. I was afraid that if I talked about it, I might jinx myself. But now it's real. It's really, really real. Other than my sister, you're the first person I've told."

"That's fantastic," Warren said, mustering the energy to sound enthusiastic. But he did not feel anything like enthusiasm. He felt dread. He could hear her displaced cats crying in the background. "Congratulations," he managed weakly. This moment, he knew, was the beginning of the end.

Actually, it turned out to be just the plain old end. "Listen," she said. "My sister is giving me her frequent flier miles, and I want to come to New York to celebrate."

"What a great idea," Warren told her.

"I want to come tonight," she said, lowering her voice. "I want you tonight, Jake. It's been so long for me, and I want you right now. I can hardly stand it."

The easy thing, Warren knew, would be to let her fly to New York and then let her figure it out for herself. Just give her a fake address, promise to meet her at the airport, anything like that. Maybe for some ordinary woman he would have done that, but he needed to handle this situation with a gentle touch. Heather deserved better. "Listen," he explained, "this is terrible timing, I guess, but I've got great news too. I just got off the phone with my agent, and I've got to fly out to the coast tonight. It looks like Ang Lee wants to do the movie. He wants to meet with me right away."

"Oh my God!" She screamed the scream of the victorious. Jake's success, Warren realized, was not some abstract thing. It was *her* success too. She envisioned Jake's seven-figure deal as the ticket to a new life. Not that Heather was a gold digger; she believed that Jake would want them to be together.

"Oh my God," she repeated, this time without the screeching. "That's so wonderful. I can't believe it. I mean, of course I can believe it, but it's so great." Then a pause. "He wants to meet with you on a Saturday?"

"He's leaving for Hong Kong on Sunday," Warren explained, "and my agent thinks he's hoping to sign a contract before he goes. It's all happening so fast, which is I guess how things go in Hollywood. Nothing happens for a long time, and then everything happens at once. I really wish I could see you, Heather, but after this is all over, we can celebrate."

"Wait a minute," she said. "Why don't I fly out to L.A. and meet you there? I bet they're putting you up in a nice hotel. I love hotels."

"I wish we could, but I'm going to be so busy," Warren said.

"Jake," she breathed. "You're only going to be busy during the day. I want to keep you busy at night."

"It's really tempting, but I need to be focused for this. If my mind is wandering, it can cost me a lot of money or I might lose control of the project. I'll call you as soon as I'm done, and we'll work something out. I can stay out in L.A. if you want to come out west, I can come to you, we can go to New York together. Whatever you want."

"Oh, Jake, I understand, but I was so hoping I could be with you tonight."

"I know. The idea is driving me crazy, but it just isn't right. But it's only a day or two." He paused for a moment. "This may sound crazy since we've never actually met in person, but I don't think two people have to be in the same room to know something like this. The truth is, I love you, Heather."

Not even a pause. "I love you, too, Jake."

"I have to run," he said, "the car is waiting for me downstairs. But I just wanted to tell you that before I go. I love you, and I will see you very, very soon."

As soon as Warren disconnected, he called his phone-service provider and canceled the account.

He had a hard time falling asleep that night. He felt kind of unhappy about the way things had turned out. Heather had been great. She'd really been the most exciting woman he'd yet found, and the relationship had lasted longer and had been more intense than any Internet relationship he had ever known. And now it was all over. Still, as bad as he felt, he knew it could not have gone any other way. He could hardly have met her, not after sending her pictures of Rick. No, it had to end. That was just how these things went.

The next day he answered a few ads, and by Sunday night he had a couple of live prospects. Warren felt a whole lot better.

—

Meanwhile, Rick's book on gender in early eighteenth-century narratives had hit the shelves, and while the slow progress of academia meant that the major journals would not review it for months, maybe even years, it had already made a splash in the profession. It was one of those rare must-read books that everyone, even those outside Rick's specialization, felt they had to account for. Warren heard the other graduate students talking about it incessantly. Rick had a lock, they said, on the Modern Language Association's first-book award. Lecture offers had begun to pour in for Rick. The administration now treated him like a big shot.

Rick started acting like a movie star. He greeted people in the hall by pointing and winking. He bought a bunch of new clothes. Before the book came out, he would scowl when he saw Warren playing Minesweeper. Now he offered a smile or some stupid encouraging remark. To balance things out, to keep the cosmos in order, Warren knew he had to heat up the stalker campaign, which he had allowed to lapse during his torrid affair with Heather.

"I was in the audience when you gave that lecture last Thursday," Warren wrote in the voice of stalking Tina, hot on the heels of a fund-raising talk Rick had delivered to the alumni association. "I like hearing you talk, but I would like to hear you cry a little too. You seem to me like your sensitive enough to cry. I sometimes think that maybe your a faggot." Warren loved to throw in little misspellings because they made the letters more frightening.

Three days after Rick received that last letter, Warren had stepped out of the English office for his lunch break when he noticed an attractive woman in her forties wandering around the hallways, casually glancing at the graduate-student mailboxes. She wore jeans and a T-shirt, and had, in Warren's opinion, a decent body. Her unremarkable brown hair was cut short, and she kept it in the kind of functional perm that Warren associated with the Midwest.

"You work in that office?" she asked Warren.

"Yeah," he said both cautiously and casually.

"Can I talk to you for a minute?"

"What about?"

She took a step forward and offered him a very professional-looking smile. "I'm a state-licensed investigator, and I'd like to ask you a few questions."

Warren studied her again. A state-licensed investigator? What the hell did that mean? "What state are you licensed in?" he asked slowly, as though avoiding stepping on something dangerous.

The answer terrified him. "Missouri."

He nodded, trying not to show his panic. "You're a private dick?" He placed a special emphasis on the last word.

"Maybe you're a public one, huh? Come on, sport. I just want to ask you a few questions."

"Shoot."

"You know this guy?" She held up a print of one of the pictures of Rick that Warren had been circulating around the Internet.

"Yeah, he's a professor here. What's this about?"

"What do you know about him? Is he married, single, or what?"

"He's single."

"He ever been to New York?"

"I don't know. Maybe for conferences or something."

"Yeah? He have a girlfriend?"

"Why, are you looking to date him?"

"You're clever, aren't you, sweetie?" Her cell phone rang. She excused herself and grunted a couple of yesses and nos and then said she'd call later. She cast a glance at Warren's lime-colored blazer and olive jeans. "That was the Jolly Green Giant on the line for you, Sprout. Wants to know where you've been."

"You insult everyone you interrogate?"

"Yeah, I do. It's a bad habit. Look, you know anything odd about this guy? He do a lot of Internet dating? That sort of thing?"

"I really can't answer these questions. It's office policy, you know. But good luck to you."

Warren returned to the office. He felt like he'd been caught shoplifting. There was no mistaking this situation. Heather had hired State-Licensed to track down Jake. How had she gotten as far as she had? Warren then remembered calling Heather from the department, the one time he'd slipped up. The PI had obviously managed to track down Heather's incoming calls.

Warren couldn't just let her alone. He couldn't have her wandering around the English department asking questions. Sure, it would make Rick look bad, but if the situation were to continue, who knew what State-Licensed might find out. He had to take action.

"Something wrong?" Edgardo asked him.

Warren had been leaning against the wall and panting. "Call security," he said. "I think Rick's stalker is in the hall."

———

Security on the South Florida State campus mainly concerned itself with chasing off local thieves, ensuring that no one violated the parking code, and protecting sorority girls who'd been drinking from fraternity boys who'd been drinking. The interrogation, Warren realized pretty quickly, was not going to look like a scene from *Law & Order.* Two meat-headed security guys escorted the PI, whose named was Jane Heart, into the departmental conference room. As department chair, Tucker figured he should be present, and they called in Rick, who had been in the middle of office hours. His door had been closed and locked, and Warren thought it took him a while for him and his pretty little student to emerge, but Rick had been okay to Warren. "Good work. You thought quick on your feet." And, for reasons Warren could not quite understand, no one seemed to object to Warren sitting in the conference room while they haphazardly tossed questions at Jane Heart.

"Am I under arrest?" Jane asked no one in particular when Rick, Tucker, and Warren walked into the room. "Or do I just have to serve detention?"

"Don't be cute," Rick said, wanting to play the tough-guy cop. Maybe this was some kind of fantasy for him.

"Can't help it," she said. "Neither can you, I see. Which is why I don't get why you want to go around breaking hearts on the World Wide Web. What gives, prof?"

Jane had volunteered her state license already, and it was lying on the conference table. Rick picked it up and stared at it. "I'm going to guess that you're not the stalker, but you want to tell me who hired you?"

"You know I can't do that. Besides, you probably have a pretty good guess, unless you make a habit of this sort of thing. And the way I hear it, you haven't exactly been stalked. You have a relationship with someone and then just drop out, and the person looks for you—I don't see it as stalking. My client, first and foremost, wanted to make sure you hadn't been killed, which she thought might be the case. She thought you'd been in a car accident or drowned in some posh Hollywood swimming pool or something. She didn't even want to listen when I introduced the asshole hypothesis."

"Your client is out of her mind," Rick said. "She's been sending me threatening notes and packages for months. And to the best of my knowledge I've never laid eyes on her or spoken with her." He picked up the print of his pic. "I don't have the first idea of how she got this picture. Whatever she's told you is a fantasy and a lie."

"To be honest, I think you're the one who's into fantasies and lies, prof. You haven't exactly been on the level with her. You lied about where you live and what you do. That's not exactly honest Internet dating, now is it?"

Rick blushed. He had never told anyone that his stalker had emerged from an Internet dating ad. "Look, I never said anything that wasn't true to her. We exchanged a few e-mails, and then she flipped. If she's telling you anything else, she's a liar. And what the hell is she doing in Missouri, anyhow? She told me she lived around here, and I'd be willing to bet that her name is not really Tina."

Jane Heart quietly licked her lips. Warren could see her assessing the situation. Maybe her client *was* crazy. This Rick guy seemed like a pretty stand-up citizen with a real job, no wife, and no obvious need for Internet shenanigans. Suppose her client had sent her on a wild goose chase? Well, Rick imagined Jane Heart deciding, she'd get paid no matter who turned out to be crazy. Case closed. No point in dragging this out.

"Okay," Jane said after a minute. "We clearly have some crossed wires going on here. I don't think my client is stalking you, but who knows? Anything is possible, and I've done my job, so how about we just call this whole thing quits and I hightail it off campus? Sound good?"

Rick looked confused. "Just tell her to leave me alone, okay? I don't care who she is or what her beef is. I just want her to leave me alone. That's it."

"I'll certainly tell her," Jane said. She picked up the picture of him and handed it back. "You hold on to this. I don't need it anymore."

———

One week later, Heather showed up in the English office. Warren had been playing Minesweeper on the computer when he saw her walk through the door, and thought for a moment to hide, but he then realized she didn't know him. She had no way of knowing what he looked like. Besides, Rick had just walked through the door only minutes before. The timing could not have been better.

Heather appeared to him even more attractive in person. She was slim, with breasts larger than her picture suggested and great-looking lips that were pressed together in grim determination. Her hair had grown out since the pictures had been taken, and she wore it up in a bun, which gave her a kind of sexy, matronly quality.

Warren unconsciously looked over to Tucker's office. The door was open and inside Rick chatted casually with the chair. Heather looked around, as if to ask someone where she might find Rick, but then spotted him herself.

"I see you, you bastard!" she shouted.

Edgardo, who had not yet noticed Heather, now turned and stared.

Rick and Tucker both looked out of the office. "Get out here, Jake," she said. "Or Rick or whatever your name really is."

Rick stood up. He and Tucker whispered a few words. The chair tried to hold him back, but Rick shook his head.

"Based on your completely inappropriate behavior, I think I can guess who you are," Rick said as he emerged. "Maybe you'll tell me what you want."

"What do I want? What do you think I want?" Heather now started to cry. "I want an explanation."

"An explanation for what?" He turned to Warren. "Call security." He then looked back at Heather. "You're going to be escorted out of here in a few minutes. I intend to have you detained until the police can deal with you. Stalking is a crime, and I just don't want to have to deal with this anymore. I guarantee you that once security gets here, I will never exchange another word with you again, so if you have something to say, I think you had better say it now."

Heather continued to cry. "I don't know why I came here," she said. "I don't know what I expected, but I can't believe you would treat me like this. Why did you tell me you loved me? Why did you say that if you were only going to disappear? And why did you tell all those lies about yourself?"

Rick shrugged. He held himself straight, smiled a little, displayed a curious confidence. "We can't have a conversation if you are going to spout fantasy. All we did was exchange a few e-mails. I never told you I loved you. I never lied to you about anything."

"What about our phone conversations, Jake?"

"My name's not Jake. You know, I think you have me confused with someone else—someone who lives in the land of make-believe. But soon the magic choo-choo will come to take you to a happy place."

"You are such a bastard," she screamed. "You think you can stand there and pretend that I'm crazy? You think you can have me arrested? For what? For wanting to talk to you? Is it a crime to find out why you tortured me?"

Warren looked at Heather with admiration. She gave a very strong performance. If he had known nothing about the situation, he surely would have believed her impassioned crying over Rick's cool indifference.

Maybe at first Rick had been a little scared. He feared she might have a gun or a knife or a hand grenade strapped to her, but now he began to sense her weakness, and he began to have a little fun. Here was this woman who had been making his life miserable for months. Maybe he thought she had it coming. "Nobody tortured you but yourself. You're pathetic. Look at you. You're a nice-looking woman. You could meet someone and have a normal life. But you go off into la-la land and make up some crazy drama that has nothing to do with anything. Before I met you, I admit you made me pretty uneasy, but now I just think you're sad. Let's see if you get a thrill stalking someone who laughs at you."

Just then two different meat-headed security guards came through the door.

"This is the woman who has been threatening me," Rick announced. "Please escort her to the security office and then call the police. I'll meet you there in a couple of minutes. I want to get the file of letters she sent to me."

"You think those letters will convict me of anything?" Heather asked. "Only if trusting a liar is a crime."

The security guards led her out the door. Warren watched her go, and then settled back into his chair, relieved. Soon it would be all over. No one had linked him to Heather and no one ever would.

Rick stood around for a minute after she had gone. Maybe he had begun to regret taunting her. It might have been satisfying at the time, but he now found himself left with the burden of having psychologically dismembered a fragile woman in public. Tucker and Edgardo and a pair of graduate students who had wandered in all half-stared at him. Rick looked away and stormed out of the office, slamming the door behind him.

"It really makes you wonder," Edgardo whispered to Warren. "I mean, how do we really know that Rick isn't the one who's crazy?"

Warren just grunted. He had already started playing Minesweeper again.

DANTE VISITS INFERNO MEDIA'S
ONLINE TECHNICAL-SUPPORT FORUM

Richard Dooling

The Dark Wood of Error Messages

Midway on my life's journey, I went astray while watching a Macromedia Flash video of a *Sports Illustrated* swimsuit model named Beatrice Portinari. When it was over, I wanted more, so I meta-searched, looking for stills and videos of her not wearing a swimsuit, and I finally found some on Inferno Media's Celebrity Skin website, where a hyperlink under the video player caught my eye. It said, "!!!Click Here for Real-Time Hot Chat with Beatrice!!!"

Right. Beatrice Portinari was probably slinking around a dance club in Cozumel with her Italian actor boyfriend, not holed up in a Silicon Alley cube farm instant-messaging with solitary cyber perverts. But I was devil-may-care, so I clicked on it anyway, and instead of caring, the devil just hosed my entire system; everything locked up—keyboard, browser, e-mail client, word processor— even the Task Manager was unreachable.

A freeze-frame of Beatrice lingered on the screen, missing a few swaths of pixels. I still had a mouse, so I clicked HELP on the menu bar and promptly got lost in a dark forest of indexed hypertext. I wandered aimlessly in the opaque, infernal syntax of the Help Underworld, where every question was answered except mine. My spirit grew heavy and I almost gave up.

Finally, the keyboard came back to life, and I used it to summon the Natural Language Answer Wizard: "This is Hell on earth! Eternal meaningless instructions leading nowhere! How do I get out of this program?"

The screen blinked and the computer had the technical equivalent of petit mal or a transient ischemic attack—flashing random commands and alerts on the screen. Then the monitor clicked, and faded to black. A split second later, it hummed like an oracle and displayed the blue screen of death strewn with white text, where terrifying hieroglyphics and cuneiform error messages spelled out the codes of doom and system fatality. My blood froze and so did my machine.

I pressed F1 on the keyboard, and a presence appeared in a small window at the lower right of my screen and hovered there in the discolored air. It was a dancing paper clip, an animated cartoon, who winked at me, made faces, and spoke to me in dialogue bubbles: "How can I help you?" "I-am-your-slave"-type stuff. I was put off by its medieval eagerness to serve me at any cost.

The paper clip did one more ta-da! and tendered more urgent, pointless offers of assistance. If the Israelites had been an ancient race of technology addicts with information sickness, they probably would have worshiped icons like this officious, hyperactive paper clip. And Moses would have banned the thing as a false idol when he came back down from Mount Server carrying the Ten Frequently Asked Questions and the Technical Support Manual.

"Whether you are shade or living man," I cried, "have pity on me!"

The paper clip wagged its tail and formed itself into antic shapes trying to draw attention to itself: "My name is Virgil," said the bubble text.

I summoned the Media Player, and Virgil the Talking Paper Clip spoke to me in streaming audio: "I've been sent by a Higher Power to be your guide. Please select a communication style from the drop-down menu of your grammar checker."

Virgil proffered a variety of style selections: casual, standard, formal, technical, or custom, with a sample of each. I clicked on "casual" and Virgil previewed my selection by reading some sample text in casual style: "I was thirty-something; I went for a walk in meatspace and got lost in a real forest. I couldn't find my ass with both hands and a pack of bloodhounds, and then a tech-support geek named Virgil showed up saying the Help Desk had sent him."

I chose "standard" and let Virgil take over.

Several Flash add-ins and dynamic Web pages loaded, after which I heard audio clips of damned souls wailing in sixty different languages. My guide explained to me that these were souls in Limbo or Purgatory on hold and waiting for technical support. The Help Desk jockey's name was Charon, and he advised that my hold time would be more than twenty minutes, but to please stay in the online queue and my call would be answered in the order received, and that meanwhile I should select the webcam option if I wanted to visit with other lost souls on hold, or sample some of Inferno Media Software's new Total Touch multimedia environments.

The cookies in my browser must have clued them in, because first up on the screen were some 3-D digital clips of Beatrice modeling on location in Maui for the *Sports Illustrated* swimsuit issue. Beach Babe City. Then I was forwarded to the First Circle Support Forum, where I went interactive with a technical-support geek named Minos, who told me to click and drag my user errors from the dialogue box and drop them on his cartoon avatar. Then he used his tail to assign me a trouble-ticket number and a slot in the Second Circle Support Forum for cybersex addicts who use their machines for carnal purposes.

Sinners of the Flesh

I joined the Sinners of the Flesh in the Second Circle Hot Chat Forum, where the carnal and the lusty betray reason to insatiable, earthbound appetites. A pop-up menu displayed a list of sinners available for private conferencing: (1) wanton Cleopatra; (2) faithless Dido; (3) lusty Francesca.

I moved my cursor over the lush Beyond True Color digital photo of Francesca in a Lycra G-string and a see-through satin slip, holding a hair dryer in her lap, just so. A .wav file opened, and a breathy woman's voice said, "I'm Francesca. I said no to eternal happiness in heaven, because I could not resist the smoldering cravings of my hungry loins. Now I'm all alone down here. Please come visit me."

I clicked hell for leather all over Francesca's icon, but another rotating banner ad kept getting in the way. Then Virgil the talking paper clip came back and told me to type my request in natural language and a virtual expert would answer it.

I typed: "I want hot chat with Francesca, or else just get me out of here and back to my desktop."

Before Virgil could answer, my time in the help queue ended and a soothing young woman's voice said: "Welcome to Inferno Media Technical Support. My name is Beatrice, and I can help you."

Unbelievable audio. Inferno Media was showing off its pride-of-the-industry 3-D Surround Palpable audio for NetHeadPhones. Stunning aural texture effects. I had Koss Quiet Zone 2000 Personal Sound System headphones with antinoise technology rigged to the latest nose-bleeding Soundblaster card, and I could feel the woman's voice, like she was sitting right next to me, or maybe she was cuddled in my lap in a red velvet sound booth.

"C'mon," I said into my headset mic, "you're not Beatrice Portinari?"

"We're not allowed to give out our last names," she said, "but my first name is Beatrice. I promise," and she threw in a throaty giggle. "Inferno Media's servers examine your cookies and search your user profile to see if you have any favorite celebrities selected, then we route you to an appropriately named tech-support person. In your case, a Beatrice. We're spread all over the country, the world actually, so we have four or five Beatrices at least, and they'll probably hire more soon because we service a lot of Beatrice Portinari fans like you. What seems to be the problem?"

I just wanted her to keep talking so I could revel in the high-end vocal audio.

"I was on one of your sites," I said, "and . . ."

"Your help options are set to auto enable," she said, "so I am retrieving our product ID number from your system registry using Inferno Media's live-update software."

Banner ads appeared in all four corners of the screen for Inferno Media products and Underworld accessories. The word *Orpheus* flashed in one of the ads, and I'd recently bought the *Black Orpheus* soundtrack online, so I had the usual curiosity about whether I'd found the best price.

Then the banner ad rotated and said "!!!Click Here!!!—If you want to hear Orpheus, the most famous musician in all of antiquity, give the performance of his life to free his wife, Eurydice, from the lascivious grasp of Bill Gates."

"Well," I said, "I was visiting one of your sites. And I—"

The ads were distracting, because now a curvaceous brunette in a skimpy black leather vest over a sheer animal print, stretch mesh, black babydoll lace chemise opened a window and said, "I'm Eurydice, please meet me in the Carnal Delights Online Shopping Boutique and see me model my Underworld lingerie. Don't look back on your way over or you won't be seeing me, Eurydice, Inferno Media's Private Pleasure Partner of the Year, modeling Inferno Media's hot, hot, *hot* selection of Underworld lingerie."

"It's okay to look at the ads," Beatrice said. "That's why we put them there. Cool pixel technology, isn't it?"

"Yeah," I said. "Nice ads."

"You were visiting one of our sites," she said, kind of singsong teasing me, like she knew most Inferno Media sites were naughty, but sometimes people like to get naughty, and so what? "Were you trying to click on the Beatrice Portinari hot chat link?"

How did she know that?

"May I assume control of your front end?" she asked.

"My what?"

I was a little embarrassed telling a female tech-support person that I had been looking for hot chat with Beatrice Portinari. I'm married, and with the aggregated consumer data banks the Web retailers access these days, she probably knew that and a lot more about me. She probably had my profile open on her screen: what sites I visit, what magazines and books I read, what music I listen to.

"Your machine, your desktop. It's just like LapLink or PCAnywhere," she said. "You just allow me to assume control of your operating system. I diagnose and inventory everything for you, then test any repairs by showing you a few more samples of our new line of Beatrice merchandise. Kind of a fun way to check your image quality. You and I can watch clips of Beatrice Portinari together, and I will adjust the flesh tone palettes until she looks just the way you like her. We can install add-ons or plug-ins together. Do you use an Inferno Media Gigapixel Beyond True Color webcam?"

"No," I said. "I don't have one."

"That's a shame," she said. "You have a nice voice. If you had an Inferno Media Gigapixel Beyond True Color webcam I could see you."

A window opened in the upper right-hand corner of my screen, and there she was. The video was even better than the audio. She sounded like she was in a red velvet sound booth, because she *was,* sitting right there in some burgundy-colored sound chamber, her skin glowing in the light of her eighteen-inch flat-panel monitor. Her face came nowhere near the perfection of Beatrice Portinari, but she was plenty good-looking everywhere else, all dolled up in a silk kimono, sitting in a Hermann Moeller chair at a desk and keyboard tray, just like I was. She was mousing away, steering the webcam so that it angled down the neckline of the kimono where her shadow-dappled cleavage filled out a scarlet lace bra.

"You can assume control of the webcam," she said. "Try out some of the new giga-resolutions on these Beyond True Color reds."

A cartoon console appeared on my screen, with a kind of virtual toggle stick. I could tilt and swivel, zoom in and out. I angled back up until I had a headshot of her in the video window. She looked up from her typing and said, "Hi, Dante. I'm Beatrice with Inferno Media's Online Technical-Support Forum, and I can help you."

Maybe it was in her job description to be warm and sincere, and if so she was the best in the business.

"See me?" she asked. Then her face collapsed into a pout. "But I can't see you, because you don't have an Inferno Media Gigapixel webcam on your machine. We have a special on them right now. Let me show you how mine works," she said. "Enlarge your video-player window and increase your pixel density."

I clicked on the control, and the window doubled in size. She came back into breathtaking focus, movie-quality stuff, but it was right there on my screen, and I could see those lean curves moving under her kimono. She put her hand on her mouse and made the camera zoom in on her mouth. Then she opened a vial of Inferno Media's Nude Bloom Bavarian Gentian Lip Gloss and smeared some on for me.

She mashed her lips together and showed me the spectacular digital video effects of the soft lights on her moist lips. "All Inferno Media lip products are designed to enhance online video effects," she added. "Free shipping if you order it before we get off." She slipped in a low laugh. "I mean, before you log off. If you were a good husband you'd buy some of this for your wife."

I knew she knew!

"Well, that's really why I came to the site," I said. "I was looking for something to buy for her."

Beatrice looked down at her screen and tapped something on the keyboard.

"It's okay if we chat while I'm checking your system," she said. "Most of the tests run automatically. Do you think your wife would like a sheer animal print, stretch mesh, black babydoll lace chemise, like the one you saw Eurydice wearing?"

"Maybe," I said. "Can I see it again?"

She assumed control of the webcam and found her own face. She smiled into the camera and said, "I can send you over to the Carnal Delights Online Shopping Boutique where you can watch Eurydice model it, or I can model it for you right here."

"You mean, you can just . . ."

She pulled back on the webcam to reveal a folding screen, back-lit by candlelight, and a rack of flimsy lingerie.

"I'll be right back," she said, and ducked behind the screen.

The banner ads started churning, and I heard a damned soul scream far off somewhere down in the lower circles.

"!!!Click Here If You Want Violence Before Sex!!!

"According to our online surveys, many of our users report heightened sexual experiences following exposure to simulated on-line violence. !!!Click Here!!!—if you want to see a 3-D streaming video of Count Ugolino gnawing the scalp of Archbishop Ruggieri in the Ninth Circle of Hell, while the violent and the bestial scald their skins in a river of boiling blood. Customized stock ticker included."

I watched Beatrice's silhouette stooping and slipping into the chemise behind the screen, then she said, "Here I come!"

"!!!Visit HarmLessLust.com!!!"

She did a turn for me and shimmied around underneath all those animal print mesh holes. Then she sauntered up close to the camera and sat down again at her keyboard.

"If you had an Inferno Media AromaMaster Olfactory add-in you could smell my Bavarian Gentian perfume."

"I could *smell* you?"

"You like?" she asked, smiling right at me. She ran the webcam over the chemise for me, slithering herself against the texture of it. "Made with the latest nanotechnology fabrics. It's fitted with over two million teledildonically controlled microscopic tongues, which you could operate for me and stimulate every nerve in my skin using TotalTouch technology."

More banner ads:

"!!!Members Only! Click Here If You Want More Violence Before Sex!!!"

"!!!Warning! You Must Be 19 Years Old to Enter the Ninth Circle of Hell!!!"

"!!!Click Here!!! if want to see Bertrand de Born, Sower of Discord Between Kinsmen, holding his own decapitated head by the hair and swinging it like a lantern!!!"

"!!!HotHotHot Chat! Right Here on Concupiscence.com!!!"

"I'll take the chemise," I said, and I clicked on the one-click order button because it kept drifting over and blocking my view of the shadow between her legs where the chemise ended and the world began.

"I fixed your video drivers," she said. "You want me to test them for you?"

"Sure," I said.

I had the video-player window wide open on my desktop, and she moved the webcam from her lips down her throat to where her chest was draped in black lace. She slipped off her right shoulder strap, and let the fabric fall away. She cupped her breast in her hand, and showed it to me.

"You like girls named Beatrice, and you like large nipples, right? Do you have an Inferno Media RoboSuck unit I can operate remotely for you?"

"A what?"

She giggled. "You are such a babe in the dark wood of error." The muzzy singsong came back into her voice. "You want me to tell you about the birds and the bees? Guys use a Millennium 2000 Customized Velvet Silicon RoboSuck unit and girls use one of these."

She pulled the webcam back for me and put a flesh-colored leather saddle on the seat of her chair, with an anatomically correct vibrator mounted on it that she said came with interchangeable heads, and a separately controlled silicone tickler at the base.

"An Inferno Media RoboThrust Satin Pleasure Saddle."

She straddled it and settled herself onto it, her sighs resounding in Surround Palpable 3-D inside my headphones. Every breath she took sounded different and more interesting than the one before it, and all I could do was listen.

"The best thing about our webcam special," she said, "is that if you order it from me, then I'm the one who helps you set it up and shows you how to use it. And right now we're offering free FedEx Next Day Delivery on all webcams if you order a RoboSuck unit or a RoboThrust Satin Pleasure Saddle for you or your partner."

She moaned softly and got comfortable on the saddle. Then she pouted in the camera and said, "I'm mad because I can't see you, or touch you. I wish we could go peer-to-peer. My ports are open, uncorrupted, and reserved for you."

"I'll take the webcam and the RoboSuck unit," I said, and clicked on the one-click order button that kept drifting into the frame and obscuring my view of her breasts. "And you'll help me set it up tomorrow night?"

She licked her lips, tilted her pelvis into the saddle, and said, "If I can wait that long."

A stylish console opened under the video-player that said, "Remote RoboThrust Satin Pleasure Saddle Dual Action Controls," and underneath were twin panels: one called "Organ Controls" (circumference, length, circumcised, uncircumcised) and the other called "Tickler Controls" (sliding scales in each column for slow-fast, soft-hard).

"Tickler frequency," she said, closing her eyes and thrusting herself against the saddle.

I clicked and dragged the sliding slow-fast control in the Tickler column.

"Now harder," she said, as she started moving herself rhythmically against it.

I slid the soft-hard control from 50 to 65.

"Yes," she said. "Like that."

Meatspace

Then I heard the baby crying.

Hell! I'd been hearing it for a while, but I thought it was just another bereft soul on hold, or the violent and the bestial scalding their skins in moats of boiling blood, but it wasn't. It was Maddy, my five-month-old daughter, and if she'd been crying for long it meant my wife, Michelle, was probably up too. I minimized all open windows, and listened for anybody moving around upstairs. Then I took the front stairs two at time without making a sound.

Michelle was asleep, the TV on with no sound. 1:34 A.M. on the digital. And Maddy had stopped crying. She cooed a few times, and I stood outside her door until I heard the rhythmic baby breaths reform themselves to the patterns of sleep.

I peeked in on Michelle again. Still out. Then I charged back downstairs and maximized the Inferno Media site window. Beatrice was gone. I was back at Inferno Media's homepage, where I saw the same button under the Beatrice Portinari video that said, "!!!Click Here for Real-Time Hot Chat with Beatrice!!!"

The only other difference on my screen was an Inferno Media Invoice and Virtual Receipt:

!!!THANK YOU FOR VISITING INFERNO MEDIA!!!

1 Millennium 2000 Customized Velvet Silicon RoboSuck unit	$79.99
1 Inferno Media Gigapixel Webcam	$299.00
1 sheer animal print, stretch mesh, black babydoll lace chemise (size = wife 1)	$49.00
1 Inferno Media Nude Bloom Bavarian Gentian Lip Gloss	$19.99
1.5 oz Inferno Media Bavarian Gentian Perfume	$34.99
1 Inferno Media AromaMaster Olfactory Add-In	$59.99

Hey! I never ordered the lip gloss! I never clicked the one-click button on the lip gloss! Nor on the AromaMaster or the perfume either!

But that wasn't the worst. $2.95 per minute for Personal Online Technical Support totaling twenty-nine minutes for $85.55! Add tax and *shipping*! The harlot vixen! FedEx First Overnight to the tune of $62.75 for 17.5 pounds of Inferno Media merchandise. The chatroom strumpet! For a grand total of $691.26 and 8 percent sales tax of $50.29 equals $741.55!

I tasted bile and my throat burned with rage. I clicked on Beatrice's !!!HOT CHAT!!! button again, and up jumped the login box asking for my username and password. I have two Inferno Media accounts in two different user profiles on my machine and I couldn't remember which one I'd used. I went with dante86 instead of dante69, and whoosh, the webcam window opened, and I was back in the burgundy sound booth with—was it Beatrice?

Beatrice 2

Instead of Beatrice, a virtual mannequin occupied her chair. Her torso, breasts, limbs, legs, hair, and face were tagged with schematics and file names: 36DD-breastanimated.gif or longlegs.jpg. She looked like a working model of Ananova, the virtual newscaster, or Lara Croft of Tomb Raider fame.

"Welcome to Inferno Media Technical Support," she said. "My name is Beatrice, and I can help you."

There was the same stunning audio, but the voice was different. It wasn't the voice of my first Beatrice.

"I just placed an online order with another Beatrice," I said, "and I need to talk to her right away."

"Please wait," she said, "while I search your user profile and history for a prior Inferno Media Pleasure Partner or Agent."

Her voice was almost as interesting as the voice of the other Beatrice, but I had a score to settle with Beatrice 1. Lip gloss! Perfume! And shipping!

"I'm sorry," Beatrice said, "you must have either logged in before under a different username, or you have never been assigned to an Inferno Media Pleasure Partner or Agent. I can assign you to a new Inferno Media Pleasure Partner now, or you may log out and reenter with a different username. Which would you like?"

I almost told her to log me out, so I could find the other Beatrice and demand my money back. Then I wondered, why not see what another Beatrice looked like first?

"Go ahead and reassign me, and I'll see if it's her," I said.

"Okay," she said. "I'll examine your live-update profiles for suggested features and preferred characteristics."

The figure filled itself in before my eyes in stunning Beyond True Color detail. Maybe the other Beatrice had indeed tuned up my machine, for in the webcam window was a moving, breathing image of Beatrice Portinari. It was her, every inch of her in all of her splendid carnality. It was no look-alike or actress, nobody else looked like her.

"Welcome to Inferno Media Technical Support," she said. "My name is Beatrice, and I can help you."

It was her voice, too, none other; it sounded just like the audio clips from the *Sports Illustrated* Maui shoot.

"Hi, Dante. My name's Beatrice. Do you use an Inferno Media Gigapixel Beyond True Color webcam?"

"No," I said. "I don't have one. That's—"

"That's a shame," she said. "You have a nice voice. If you had an Inferno Media Gigapixel Beyond True Color webcam I could see you. We have a special on them right now. Let me show you how mine works."

CODE

Bruce Sterling

Even in death, Louis's bulk had wedged him firmly into his work chair.

Van felt swift, unthinking rage. How could Louis do this to him? Van had been working on a software patch all week, code that only Louis would appreciate.

But Louis's bearded face had gone slack, and his waxy hide was mottled and bluish. The little office—with its scrawled whiteboards, pinned wallboards, a host of colored Post-Its—held the reek of a large dead animal. Van had entered a room with a corpse.

Van leaned across the body and punched up www.google.com on Louis's glowing screen.

<<Discover dead body proper legal procedures>>

The search engine spat up results. An exhumation carried out in Argentina by a human rights commission. A treatise on Jewish funerals. Frantic paranoia about the Global Traffic in Human Organs.

Van required immediate relevance. He surfed to www.AskJeeves. com.

<<I just found a dead body in the office. What should I do?>>

The response was broadband-swift.

"Where can I buy furniture for my office?" Jeeves said, proffering an e-commerce button.

Louis's office door opened and Julie the receptionist stepped in with a clipboard. "Hey, Louis, I need you to . . ." She stopped, and looked at the two of them, Van standing and fitfully typing, Louis fatally slumped. "What's wrong?"

"Louis is dead."

Julie raised her brows behind her rimless glasses. "No! Really?"

"Yeah. Really."

"So what are you doing?"

"I'm asking Jeeves."

"Oh. Okay." Julie stepped closer, quietly shutting the door. Although Van saw Julie the receptionist without fail every working day, he did not know her last name. Julie seemed to have a ready smile for him, for pretty much every male geek infesting the building, really, but Van had merely managed a polite nod, the occasional howdy hey y'all. Since Julie didn't write code, there was no real reason for her to ever register in Van's awareness.

"Has Vintelix ever had a workplace fatality before?" Van asked her. "You should know that, right?"

"Who, me?" said Julie, clutching the clipboard to her shallow, floppy-tied chest. She stared at the looming white cotton of Louis's XXXL T-shirt. "I've never even *seen* a dead guy! I mean, not all close and intimate."

"Well, we've got to take steps to deal with this."

"Oh, sure," she said gamely, "I mean yeah, okay, whatever."

However, no immediate useful tactic came to Van's throbbing mind. He couldn't get over the fact that it was *Louis* that was dead. "Louis was such a good guy," Van offered painfully. "He got me this job."

"Oh, sure, Louis hired me, too! Louis and I used to play Quest for Britannia online together. He was Lord Melchior and I was Dejah Thoris. Hey, Van, shouldn't we call the cops?"

Van ran a hand through his hair. "Why bother? I'd bet the cops will show up here no matter *what* we do."

That was an evil thought. The two of them exchanged significant glances.

Soon they were on their knees together, rummaging through the desk.

Cigar-burned and boot-battered, Louis's desk was a relic from some oil-drilling company with Texas-sized notions of desktop real estate. The massive oaken desk suited the larger-than-life spread of a longhaired three-hundred-pound Texan hacker. Louis got away with this eccentricity because he was Vintelix employee number 3. Besides, it was an open secret that Louis kept all his drugs in the desk.

In the back of the left third drawer, Van and Julie discovered a brown cardboard box, taped over with ancient, peeling underground cartoons. To judge by the rattling mess of pills, the dope habits of Louis's vanished youth had long since faded to a galaxy of pain-killers, blood-pressure nostrums, and heart medicine. Louis had been eating these pills with the debonair carelessness that was his signature: a relaxed contempt for the stuffy medical authorities, or utter, pigheaded, suicidal stupidity, you could pretty well take your pick.

Louis's cardboard box also contained a folded sheet of paper. The sheet bore hundreds of tiny repeated motifs, perforated like postage stamps: little colorful dancing bears. A dozen of them had been neatly clipped from the blotter paper's lower edge, with something like toenail scissors.

Van nodded, his heart sinking. "That must be Louis's acid."

"Louis did *acid?*"

"Of course Louis did acid! He was a Deadhead!" A fatal octopus of cold reality gripped Van with crushing force. Because Louis was dead, and Louis was the *boss.* Louis was the guy in the company who *got it about code,* and protected the coders from the suits. They hadn't even removed the poor guy's body yet, and already he was leaving a great big Louis-sized hole.

When Julie finally spoke again, she was using her receptionist's voice, as bright, phony, and cheery as injection-molded plastic. "Let's get out of here now, okay? Because I'm really getting creeped out."

Van lifted the battered cardboard box, a coffin of hopes. He put it on the desktop. It radiated FATAL ERROR in its fat-old-hippie defiance.

"I'm just trying to protect the company," Van told her. "It would look pretty bad for the company if somebody else found a lot of acid."

"Well, we'd better tell Darren that he's died," Julie said. "Because Darren gets mad in a hurry whenever he's, like, left out of the loop."

It made good sense to inform the CEO right away. Clearly someone had to be told, and with Louis dead, there wasn't any higher authority in Vintelix than Darren. Van examined the perforated spreadsheet grid of LSD and swiftly calculated a value of 285 hits. Properly distributed, 285 hits of acid was enough to send every single person in the company into the Texan prison system. It really wouldn't be healthy to screw this situation up.

"Okay, Julie, I'd better go tell the boss. You get rid of this dope."

"Let *me* go tell Darren. *You* get rid of the dope."

Julie wasn't handling this logically. Frustrated in a noble ambition, Van felt a crazy urge to slug her, even though violence never solved anything around the office except in marathon Quake sessions. Keep a cool head, he thought. Just reason it out, there's a solution here. "Are we going to stand here and argue about dope?"

Julie lifted both her hands, stepping back, face pale. "Hey, I never even touched that dope! You're the guy holding the dope."

"Okay, I've got it." Van produced his Swiss Army knife, opened the scissors, and neatly bisected the sheet. "Now we'll *both* get rid of the dope. And we'll both tell Darren. How about that: you and me. Are you cool with that?"

Julie tucked her share of colored paper in the back of her clipboard. "I'm cool with it if you're cool with it."

———

The two of them jointly briefed the CEO. Darren quickly alerted the Vintelix security guy, an ex-cop who usually hung out in a glass guard-shack, pretending to study the video monitors. Thrilled to earn his salary for once, the security guy rumbled into action, and appropriate steps took place.

Four medics in EMS jumpsuits took Louis away forever, on a big, sturdy medical roller cart. They were quiet and tactful about it, as if they did this sort of thing every day, as Van rather imagined that they must.

People didn't confront sudden death every day, but there was scarcely an Austinite alive who hadn't held drugs and stayed cool at some point. Van and Julie had broken the awful news without a hitch. Carrying huge amounts of drugs on their persons had somehow chilled them out. Seeing their stony faces and unnatural calm, Darren had compassionately insisted that Van and Julie take the rest of the day off. Maybe, Darren urged, they might contemplate even taking off a whole weekend.

A mournful hush fell over the Vintelix offices: long before the body left the premises, every last soul in the building knew the sad news through e-mail.

Cold waves of disorientation had Van queasy. But he really couldn't call the trauma a surprise. It had been obvious to him from day one that Louis was a waddling time bomb. Van had been a fresh graduate in computer science when Louis had hired him. One look at his new boss in the private sector had sent Van scampering to join a gym. Guys of Louis's generation had never gotten it about the work hazards of using computers. They still thought that computers were cyber magic, something like Day-Glo mushrooms, or maybe unicorns. Now, three years later, Louis was freshly dead of a major coronary, while Van could bench-press 180 pounds.

Congratulating himself on his mature foresight didn't make Van feel any better about his immediate future, though. Without Louis around to ride herd and grind code, Vintelix could easily slide straight off the edge into dot-bomb hell, and all Van's shares would be toilet paper. Sure, there were high-tech firms hiring all over town, but what a waste!

Chased from the glass-and-limestone premises where he commonly spent eighty hours a week, Van walked home alone, brooding and shaken.

Van occupied an efficiency four blocks away from the Vintelix compound. The graceless little apartment suited his purposes, since it had a broadband DSL connection and was close to the gym. Van had no pets, no chairs, and no curtains. Lacking forks and knives, he commonly ate with plastic chopsticks from the Korean grocery next door. The utter bareness of his dwelling place had never bothered Van, for frills were of no relevance to him, and he commonly ate and slept at work, anyway. Van owned only three primary possessions: a large couch, a large computer, and a large cable TV. He slept on a futon under his computer—a rather less cozy futon than the one he slept on at work.

Van turned on the lights, killed a large roach, and logged on. He was too upset to do any coding work for Vintelix, so he thought he might amuse himself with his hobby, doing unpaid coding for a Linux project. First, of course, his e-mail. Van waded through the spam and found e-mail waiting from Julie. He discovered with vague interest that her full name was Julie Woertz. Julie's e-mail offered an IRC channel. Van found Julie ready to chat.

"People around the office say you're cool," Julie typed cautiously. "They say you always bring lots of beer to the office parties."

"And???," Van parried. He was a generous patron of the company's bashes. It was easier than making small talk. Van was Vintelix employee number 26. If he cashed out some stock, he could bring a truckload of beer.

"And, so, you don't seem like a guy who really needs to have two hundred hits of acid."

"143," Van corrected automatically.

"So I wanted to ask you something. If that's all right. May I have it, please?"

Van logged in to the Vintelix intranet, found the page for Julie Woertz, got her home phone number, and called her.

"Hello?" she said, unsurprised.

"First, tell me why you want that stuff."

"So, do you still have it?"

"Yeah. I've got it."

"Well, why didn't you just trash it in the Dumpster like the rest of the pills and all?"

"I dunno," Van admitted. "A hundred and forty-three doses of acid is kind of impressive. I haven't seen that much drugs since I was in junior high school."

"But you do really think it's LSD? This paper's all yellow and old. Some website says that LSD loses its potency."

"Could be. Who knows?"

"But if it's really LSD and it's really still okay, well, I got some people in my eBay trading club who sound really, really interested."

"Julie, why do you want to sell acid on eBay? That doesn't make any sense to me. Louis never sold anybody acid. It seems kind of, I dunno . . . disrespectful."

"Hey, what's wrong with eBay?" Julie said defensively. "People love me on eBay! I got a great eBay reputation. But, you know, if they got some acid from me and it was just *no good,* then that would be *really humiliating.*"

"Well, what's the use of acid? I took Ecstasy a couple of times in high school. Maybe you want to dance, but you can't do anything worthwhile."

"Okay, fine, but it's sure dorky to just trash this paper when my net friends really want some. That just seems so . . . lame." She paused. "Hey, wait a sec. My webcam's on. Why don't you use my webcam?"

Van courteously found his own webcam, blew gritty dust off the unit, untangled its cables, and set it up. Then he followed her instructions and clicked on to Julie's cam site. Soon they were gazing at blinky screen images of each other as they talked together on the phone.

Julie was wearing a sexy black wig. Small, polite, and efficient, Julie had always looked to Van like a grocery clerk. In her webcam getup, she looked like a grocery clerk in a sexy black wig.

"So, you have a lot of fans for this home webcam action?" Van speculated, studying her stained wallpaper and peeling anime posters.

"I usually forget that it's on," Julie admitted. "I just get used to it, since it's so much like being a receptionist." She smoothed her wig. "Mostly, I do a kind of role-playing game. I kind of write little fantasy skits and performances. Like a Cindy Sherman art thing. You know Cindy Sherman?"

"She's a big Web logger, right?"

"Well, uh, no, not really." Julie plucked her sheet of acid paper from her purse. "So listen, Van: I had an idea. If I ate some of these to see if they still work, would you help me out? Like a quality test. I'm thinking that I could just stay on the cam here, and you could just kind of watch me."

"How many of those are you planning to eat?" he hedged.

"What do they call these little paper things, 'tabs'? They look really small. I was thinking maybe just four or five. Is that a big deal for you? You don't even have to get out of your chair, okay? You can just kind of click in on me and make sure that I'm, you know. Whatever."

Van sensed himself sliding gently into deep water. "Why are you picking on me for this?"

"Because nobody else knows that we have a ton of acid! You don't want me to *tell* anybody else, do you?"

Van gave himself a bump on the head with the flat of his hand. "Oh, right! Sure. Sorry."

"So is that cool with you? Because if it's not cool with you, you can just say so. I'll understand."

"How about you eat just one."

"Well, okay, but that'll probably be pretty boring. I mean, I'm not going to dress up and perform, or anything." She sighed. "Even when I do, nobody logs on."

"Well, I'm game." Van glanced at his sports watch. "I've gotta go do a few sets at the gym around ten P.M., but that's like three hours from now. That should be plenty of time. I'll just put you on speakerphone now, and get in a little coding on my X-Windows while you're doing, you know, whatever."

Office doings gave them a natural topic for conversation, but Van lacked much interest in Julie's eager gossip about who was up, down, and in and out among the company's suits. Like the rest of the Vintelix coders, Van had always prided himself on the fact that he was technically indispensable.

Within an hour, Julie grew bright and elated, and began to complain and unload through her flickering video in the corner of Van's attention. She told tales of woe against her inconsiderate hippie-chick roommate. She expressed dissatisfaction with the engine of her used car. She hearkened back repeatedly to her miserable childhood in a small West Texas town among some clan of Southern Baptists.

Julie's well-meaning parents had committed the grave mistake of buying her a computer because Julie was making straight A's. A single day's exposure to the Internet had revealed to Julie that her parents knew nothing about anything that mattered. Neither did her schoolteachers. Some slow but terrific rupture had occurred. Julie had ended up in Austin, the traditional destination for pretty much any Texan who was throughly shaken up and not yet nailed down.

Two hours later, Julie was ranting like she'd gulped two Starbucks super-grandes. She kept losing track of the webcam entirely, bolting and scampering out of camera range into the depths of her apartment, where she raided her closet for a tatty eBay finery of poodle skirts and feather boas.

To "keep him occupied," as she put it, Julie blasted MP3 files. Like many Austinites, Julie fancied herself quite the music aficionado. Julie and her pirate net-club of world music enthusiasts were into Congolese pygmy nose flutes and Bulgarian choral classics. Van didn't care much for music, especially the kind requiring anthropological liner notes. As far as he could figure it, Julie's "music collection" was a completely random jumble of files. But as long as it was different from local radio, that seemed to be fine with her.

At 10:00 P.M., Van went down to the gym for his customary late-night workout, for Julie had vanished from the camera, and the death of Louis was weighing painfully on Van's mind. The gym had become a major emotional refuge for Van, even though Van was not at all a fan of lifting weights, or even a fan of gyms. Van pumped iron because this was the only form of activity that made him stop thinking about code. Jogging and bicycling were better exercise, but they were far too dangerous for Van: in his usual abstracted haze, he could very easily fly off the limestone cliffs of Austin's hike-and-bike trails. But twenty curls with a barbell were always enough to turn his arms to smoldering rubber, and to thoroughly empty his mind.

Van did not "keep in shape." The gym guys who were really shapely tended to be gay. Van wasn't particularly strong, either. Genuine weight lifters, those squinty, bearded guys who were seriously strong, were about eight feet around in the belly. Van wouldn't have minded looking sexy and picking up some women, but he simply had no time. Van was so busy coding that he didn't have time to pick up food, much less women. He didn't even have time to pick up his paychecks.

So the many full-length mirrors at Big Sam's showed him a silent geek, with thick glasses, a funny-looking nose, and cheap, infrequent haircuts. Van was pretty much content to look like what he was: a man that nobody ever took any trouble over.

After an hour and a shower, Van returned home with his gym bag. He found Julie wandering the streetlit pavement, clutching an unopened Diet Coke. Julie had a fixed grin and her dilated eyes were as black and shiny as the buttons on a Sony boombox.

"I lost you, I lost you," she told him earnestly. "I got worried."

"What are you doing here?" he said.

"I got your address from the company website and drove over." She gestured glassily at her rusty Toyota. "But there's something wrong with my steering wheel now. It feels kind of . . . melty."

Van took the warm Coke from her hand, placed it in his gym bag, and examined her with care. She was still in her work clothes, but she had put on flipflop sandals over her stocking feet and had yanked on a pullover, backward. Van felt that he was truly seeing Julie Woertz for the very first time. She was small, frail, vulnerable, and completely stoned.

"My apartment's kind of messy," he told her. "But you better come up for a while."

"Is that cool with you?"

"Oh, sure, I'm cool, we'll just hang out," he told her vaguely. "There's usually something good on the Nature Channel this time of night."

He escorted Julie up the stairs and into his efficiency. "Wow," she said, her dinner-plate eyes examining the bare, constricting walls. "This is so . . . snug."

Van turned on the lights and pursued the vermin into hiding. He seated Julie carefully on the couch, which was a nice one, since it was the second-most expensive choice at a local furniture chain. He placed the remote in her hands. He then fetched his laptop and sat down companionably.

"You shouldn't Web surf when you have a guest," Julie told him, struggling to unfix her stony grin. "That's against the rules."

"What rules?"

"That book, *The Rules,* by Sherrie Schneider?"

Van clicked up amazon.com.

<<*The Rules: Time Tested Secrets for Capturing the Heart of Mr. Right* by Ellen Fein, Sherrie Schneider.

<<Customers who bought this book also bought:

<<*The Real Rules: How to Find the Right Man for the Real You* by Barbara De Angelis

<<*Secrets About Men Every Woman Should Know* by Barbara De Angelis

<<*The Rules II: More Rules to Live and Love By* by Ellen Fein, Sherrie Schneider

<<*The Code: Time-Tested Secrets for Getting What You Want from Women Without Marrying Them!* by Nate Penn, Lawrence LaRose>>

Van clicked twice and immediately purchased both *The Rules* and *The Code* for overnight delivery.

"Hey Julie, what was that other one you were talking about? Cindy Sherman?"

But Julie had realized that the object in her grip was a remote control, and she was eagerly channel surfing.

"Ohmigod!" she squealed. "It's *The Barretts of Wimpole Street*! This is like my third-favorite movie! Ohmigod it's Norma Shearer! Look at her hair, I had a wig just like that once!"

Van did a movie search.

<<The Barretts of Wimpole Street (1934)

<<Starring: Fredric March, Norma Shearer

<<Director: Sidney Franklin

<<Synopsis: Poet Robert Browning successfully woos invalid writer Elizabeth Barrett in this glossy historical romance. Fans of old-fashioned Hollywood romance may find that handsome production values compensate for occasionally draggy story.>>

Julie was transfixed. Long, enraptured moments passed, broken only by her intakes of breath and the gentle clicking of Van's ThinkPad. "My God," Julie breathed at last. "I'm getting into this *so much!*"

With occasional glances upward, Van watched the movie enough to catch its drift. It was a period chick flick, about a sick girl stuck at home, whose situation turns around when some good-looking con artist shows up and hands her a line of artsy bullshit.

"How about some popcorn, Julie?"

"I don't think I'm hungry." She began to tremble.

Van went to his futon, fetched off his musty blanket, and carefully wrapped her up.

"I'm afraid of dying, just like she was," she muttered. "I just don't want to die all alone."

"You're not dying. You're very alive and safe here."

"I saw a dead man today. If you hadn't been there, trying to fix it, I would have just completely freaked out. I just would have started screaming. I don't know how I would have ever stopped."

"Nice movie, huh? Handsome production values. How about a nice cup of Korean green tea?"

She hugged the blanket closer. "I'm having a really long day," she whispered, and began to sniffle.

He hadn't expected to see Julie crying. The crying thing turned him completely inside out. It hit him like a match on oil-soaked rags.

The darkest level of his psyche burst into sullen blue flames. Those tears meant she was helpless. Just like the handsome actor on the screen, he could hand this trapped, drug-addled girl any line he pleased, and she would have no choice but to nod and blink and hope for the best, and then he could do absolutely anything he wanted to her.

The crazy feeling subsided, as quick, sudden, and evil as a smash of glass and a midnight car alarm, but then there it was: she had come into focus for him. There was a woman in his life.

He sat down, picked up her hand, and patted it.

—

When they returned to work next morning, late, together, in her car, and with Julie still in yesterday's clothes, there could only be one logical conclusion. It was true that they had been sleeping together, since Van had bagged a couple of hours upright on the couch. Julie hadn't managed any sleeping. She claimed that she just felt "clear" and "kind of peaceful." Once in her work station, she slipped right back into the routine. Although when word got out in e-mail, absolutely everybody knew.

Darren called Van in for a conference. Darren was tall and handsome and probably gay, and got a lot of play in the Austin tech press. He was on the road all the time, selling the Vintelix vision to the distant venture gods of Redmond and Silicon Valley.

Darren was in a serious pinch because of Louis's sudden demise. The loss of a key programmer made it harder to meet shareholder expectations, to keep up market momentum, and to manage that special Vintelix buzz. Unlike most of the other coders, Van had some coherent idea of what Louis had been up to. So despite the fact that he was only employee number 26, Van found himself with most of Louis's work on his hands, plus a raise in salary.

Then came the obligatory "sandwich treatment," with broad hints that Van should dress more appropriately for his new, exalted station in Vintelix management. Inappropriate relationships with female Vintelix personnel were of particular concern to Darren. Van departed with a final lacquer of praise: a boost in his stock options and a new and more meaningless job title.

Van spend the rest of the day and most of the night going over Louis's code. The spaghettiware was even worse than he'd imagined. Louis had always treated the Vintelix code just like his own baby: in a way, the Vintelix code *was* Louis's own baby. It was the only baby Louis had ever had.

By one A.M. Van had arrived at a game plan: outsource everything in sight. Louis had always hired people on instinct, but Louis was the kind of guy who would hire people he played Dungeons and Dragons with. Coders who really got it were worth twelve of anybody else. So even if they were upset by a reorg, all the hardcore guys would come around when they saw some real progress made. In sum, there was probably nothing wrong with Vintelix that a total and silent hacker revolution couldn't somehow cure behind the scenes.

Van was hauled from his bed at eight A.M. to accept an express delivery of books. *The Rules* and *The Code* had arrived. Next day, while he oversaw the transfer of his own hardware to a new office more suitable to a "senior technology coordinator," Van examined *The Code.* Unfortunately, the book was merely a series of lame jokes, featuring no actual data on exploiting women for sex and not paying.

The Rules, however, was a work of deadly seriousness. Mostly, it was about phone calls.

The Rules was bitter, life-and-death, stripped of all sentimentality. It was about surviving, and protecting children, among a race of large, brutal, half-blind creatures who would exploit you without conscience and could easily beat you to a pulp. Most everything in *The Rules* made a lot of sense to Van. The thing was more than a self-help book: basically, it was an operating system. The work fired his imagination and reset his agenda.

Van went home early—at a mere 7:00 P.M.—and picked up the phone. Then he put it back down, and logged on to Julie's webcam, instead. Much as he had expected, Julie had thoughtlessly left the camera plugged in. She was carefully painting her toenails, reading a woman's magazine, and almost literally hovering over her phone.

Van captured and froze a webcam frame and blew it up for closer study. Julie's magazine was *Cosmopolitan*. The magazine featured a shapely young blonde in a blue reptile bikini top. The cover text, though blurry on the screen, was still legible. *Make Him All Yours: Play Cosmo's Fantasy Game with Him Tonight and Win His Undying Love. Man-Melting Massage. 97 Sexy Date Looks. The Confessions Issue!*

Van dialed her number. He saw her scramble for the phone in a fury, upsetting her nail polish, face alight with desperate hope.

"Hello, this is Van."

"Hello, Van," she said with polite indifference.

The previously unseen hippie roommate rushed into Julie's room. Julie emitted a silent scream of triumph, waving her fingers frantically. The roommate, enraptured, leapt up and down in sympathetic glee.

Van examined his stack of notes and cleared his throat. "Julie, listen. I need to ask a favor of you. I'm sure that you value your time and have a very crowded and fulfilling social life. However, I'd be truly grateful if you would join me tonight . . . *to shop for clothes.*"

"What did you say?"

Had he overdone it? She seemed stunned.

"Julie, I need a new wardrobe. I just got a promotion. I feel uneasy about my new role and I depend on your judgment and support. I'm sure your unique insights will help me fit in among the top echelon of the company."

"You're not mad at me for freaking out on acid in your living room? Ohmigod, I wish I'd never done that to you. I felt so embarrassed, I just could have died."

Van thumbed rapidly through his briefing cards. Here it was: the Self-Esteem Crisis. "Okay, maybe that was a little indiscreet. But frankly, I found it provocative and exciting. It was a bold move from a woman who knows what she wants from life." He leaned back. "So, Patagonia closes at nine, right? Can you come and pick me up in your car? And bring us something to eat."

"Okay, sure, right! My God, Van, we'd better hurry."

"You're saving my life here, Julie. You're a treasure." As he hung up, a net search hit pay dirt in the browser window. It was some English-major site, dating back to the early 1990s, when the Web had still been full of academics. Public-domain stuff, old poetry.

This Browning woman didn't seem to have much going on: a lot of thees and thous. Van spooled down the screen until something in the spinning text caught his eye.

>   <<A shadow across me. Straightway I was 'ware,
>   So weeping, how a mystic Shape did move
>   Behind me, and drew me backward by the hair:
>   And a voice said in mastery, while I strove,—
>   "Guess now who holds thee?"—"Death," I said. But, there,
>   The silver answer rang,—"Not Death, but Love.">>

He hit it with a bookmark. Plenty of time to decode that one later.

THE FACE IN THE GLASS

Paul Hond

Byrne switched off the engine and checked himself in the rearview mirror. Already he looked different. His act had changed him, deepened his beauty. His mouth—the finely carved lip (like a woman lying on her back, as his brother once said), the tiny divots above and below, put there, pressed there, as if by a finger to clay—had been refigured, sensualized to a point of anguish: he touched it as he would a wound, with awe and sadness. The nose, hanging nobly above, appeared smooth as a slope of marble, aloof to the lower appetites. His high cheekbones tapered delicately to the grim outline of his jaw; and when the light caught his chin there were copper sparks, bits of wire that glinted fiercely, the needles of the noonday sun.

The radio reports said that investigators had no solid leads, but were interested in a dark green sedan with Virginia plates.

Byrne's car was blue.

And by now, the weapon—a Colt .45 "Defender"—would be sunk at the bottom of the river: he'd chucked it off the Powhatan bridge, right out his window as he drove north on Mountain Road. There had been no other motorists in sight.

Byrne touched the rim of his sunglasses; he had yet to look at his eyes.

Cars pulled in and out of the lot: in the mirror Byrne could see the traffic pass on the highway. His Virginia tags felt conspicuous to him, here in Pennsylvania; if the feeling persisted he might have to ditch the car. At the very least he would have to avoid gas stations and motels. Luckily he had a gas can in the trunk.

Byrne removed his sunglasses, slowly, like a thief revealing stolen jewels: two cold blue eyes stared back at him. Byrne felt adrenaline, as though he were confronting an enemy. He then tried to admire himself in the mirrored lenses of the glasses, but his hand was shaking, causing the image to blur. This alarmed Byrne, who was susceptible to omens. He willed the tremor to stop.

He got out of the car; his knees almost buckled, and he had to put his hand on the roof to steady himself. He closed his eyes and breathed deeply.

He moistened his lips and ground the tip of one heavy workboot into the asphalt; then he kicked a pebble and watched it skip. It went much farther than he'd expected, as if it had come alive. A good sign. Heartened, he followed the smell of bacon to the entrance of the diner. Byrne was a vegetarian, not crazy, but he did believe in treating his body as a temple, and objected to unhealthful foods. At the moment, though, he wasn't hungry.

He pushed the glass door, taped to which was a flat cardboard jack-o'-lantern. Byrne did not look at its eyes. In the vestibule he noticed a bucket containing two umbrellas, even though it wasn't raining.

He was then struck with the thought that she might not be there. What then? Where would he go?

He walked past the cashier's station and looked around the place. The cushions of the booths were the sharp orange of American cheese when it has been sitting too long, and the lacquered wood-paneled walls had reddish tones that made Byrne think of light going through a bottle of cola.

He smelled pancake syrup, a cloying sweetness on the edge of a waft of meat; it reminded him, obscurely, of his mother's sick-room. . . .

He spotted her.

She was seated alone in a booth by a window, toying with buttons on a miniature jukebox that was mounted to the table. There were two cigarettes crushed out in her ashtray, and she was smoking another. The ashtrays were really just fancy pieces of tinfoil.

Byrne shrugged his shoulders under his old denim jacket and blew air into his cupped hands. Grinning faintly, he approached the table.

She looked just as her photo had promised: a big girl with a big heart. Her name was Carly. She had wide green eyes and dirty blond hair to her shoulders, styled in a perm. She wore white tennis shoes, tight black exercise pants cut out at the ankles like stirrup socks, and an oversized sweater of white, green, brown, and red, depicting what appeared to be a reindeer in the snow. Byrne had chatted with her online five or six times. She'd said she was twenty-four—a year younger than Byrne—but she seemed much older, sodden with television and disappointment. Next to her, Byrne felt ageless.

"Carly?" he said.

"Yes?" Carly looked up at him, and her eyes glittered.

"It's me," Byrne said. "Kyle." He gave a nervous, disarming laugh.

"Kyle?"

"Mind if I join you?"

Carly hastily put out her cigarette as Byrne sat down across from her.

"You don't look the same in person," she said with coy suspicion.

Byrne stroked his face. "Must be the whiskers," he said. He took a spoon in his hand and twirled it idly. "Hope you're not disappointed."

"I wouldn't think so," Carly said. "Are you?"

"Hardly," said Byrne. He had a soft, gentle voice. "I've been thinking about you the whole ride. All those things we have in common."

"Like what?" said Carly, leaning forward on her elbows.

"All those things. Like how you love animals, and hiking." Byrne smiled. "And movies."

"And going places," Carly said.

"And going places."

"If you could go anywhere in the world, where would it be?"

"Right here," said Byrne.

Carly smiled, blushed. "I was thinking more like Barbados, or South America. There's a lot of places I want to go."

Byrne glanced at his image in the concave side of the spoon. He had never been on an airplane. He was deathly afraid of them.

"You hungry?" Carly said, with some urgency, as if afraid of losing his attention. "Everything's good here."

Byrne noticed her hands. She had a ring on every finger, and her nails were bitten down. One ring had a small silver crucifix.

"An orange juice, maybe," said Byrne. He fished some quarters from his pocket.

"Oh, the orange juice is really good here," said Carly. She signaled for a waitress. "They squeeze it fresh."

Byrne fed the jukebox as Carly ordered juice for Byrne and a slice of pie for herself.

"Pick some songs," Byrne said.

"Okay," said Carly, happy as a girl at the fair. "I always play the same songs."

A song came on, something countryish that Byrne didn't know.

They talked for a while. Carly wanted to learn more about Byrne's work as an artist's model. Byrne told her that his job was to pose naked while college students drew him.

"You mean, totally naked?" said Carly.

Byrne laughed. "It's not porn or nothing like that."

"I know," Carly said, blushing. "But still, I mean, did you ever, you know—get excited or anything?"

"No," said Byrne. He wasn't smiling now. He toyed with the spoon again. "Nothing like that."

"Did I embarrass you?" Carly said. "I'm sorry."

Byrne looked around, suddenly worried that Carly had had someone follow her, to make sure that Byrne looked okay. But all he saw was a bunch of fat yokels eating scrambled eggs and sausage: a few families, some old gray-haired couples. Somewhere in the room a baby was crying.

"So what do you want to do?" said Carly. "You get to decide, since you came all this way."

"Doesn't matter to me," said Byrne, turning his attention back to her. "But first I need to figure out where I'm staying."

"I told you in my e-mail that you could stay with me," said Carly, uncapping a tube of lip balm. She applied it in slow strokes, working her lips together. Then she returned it to her shiny black handbag, which she kept on her lap like a puppy.

"Are you sure you don't mind?" said Byrne.

"No," said Carly. "Why would I?"

Byrne thanked her and ran his hand through his hair.

When they were finished, Byrne paid the bill. Then they went outside to their cars.

Carly drove a white hatchback. Byrne followed her. The day was cold and blue. Byrne felt a wave of nausea as he drove the unfamiliar road, thinking that at any moment a patrol car would appear in his mirrors. But what if he *were* stopped; what could they do to him? What evidence did they have?

Byrne sucked his lip. There were too many cars. He was grateful when Carly turned onto a back road.

The trees were in fiery form, stunned and brilliant as the plumes of wild turkeys.

After a mile, though, Byrne wondered if he was being led astray.

Carly then turned on her blinker and slowed.

Her house was hidden from view; a mailbox on the roadside announced its presence. Byrne followed Carly into a gravel driveway, at the end of which was a white, box-shaped house with lime-colored shutters. The neighboring houses were obscured on either side by a kind of curtain of field herbs and thin, crooked trees, with leaves of pink and gold.

Byrne parked behind Carly in the driveway. He got out of the car, opened the trunk, and removed his overnight bag. The small front lawn was the color of hay, and matted, as if a board had lain upon it all summer.

Carly led the way to the front door; three ears of Indian corn hung above the brass knocker.

"This was my grandparents' house," said Carly. "I was living in an apartment, but then my grandmother died, and she left me the house. The deer come right up to the back door."

They went inside. The carpet in the living room was the green of young corn husks, pale and cool-looking; the sofa was of gold velour, the end tables white with glass tops. There were family photos on the tables.

Byrne then heard the rattle of a dog shaking itself, and in the next moment a brown-and-white spaniel came jingling in from the kitchen.

"Georgie!" Carly cried. "Look who's here!"

Georgie arrived trembling at Byrne's feet, sat obediently, and looked up at the stranger with what seemed like human eyes. He barked twice.

"Hi, Georgie," Byrne said. He stooped and offered the back of his hand. Georgie licked it, then sniffed Byrne's bag.

"I'd better let him out," Carly said. "Then we'll get you set up." Byrne waited as Carly let Georgie out through the back door.

The spare bedroom had a single bed with a sky-blue spread on it. On the white wooden desk was a computer, its screen saver showing schools of fish swimming perpetually in both directions. Every so often, a fish would be upside down.

Byrne entered and set his bag on the floor. Carly stood in the doorway. On the dresser was a painted ceramic dog, the same breed as Georgie.

Byrne nodded at the computer. "Is that where you write me from?" he said.

"Uh-huh."

"Mind if I check my e-mail?"

Carly hesitated. "Why?" she said. "Are you expecting a message?"

Byrne laughed, to deflect what he took as her suspicion that he was communicating with other women. "No," he said. "I just like to check it."

"Me too," said Carly, striving to meet him. "It makes my day sometimes."

Byrne regarded the bookcase, which held an old encyclopedia, black-bound with faded gold letters. He pulled out the second volume—B for Byrne—and opened it to a random page, thinking that he might alight on some guiding word or idea. There was an illustrated diagram entitled WHAT AN AUSTRALIAN CAN DO WITH A BOOMERANG. Below was a caption: *The Australian "blackfellow" can make his boomerang do all these things.* Byrne tried again and found a picture of a Burmese pagoda that was built on a boulder that overhung a steep chasm: it was said to rock gently in the wind. He read a line about the bazaars of Mandalay that were thronged by a "curiously mixed population of Mohammedans, Jews, Hindus, Chinese, and tribesmen from the hills, with many British soldiers from the nearby cantonment." Byrne then turned to the first page, whose initial entry was "Baby Care." Under a photo of a young mother playing with her baby was a caption, part of which Byrne slowly read aloud: " '. . . and his skin absorbs the sun's ultraviolet rays, which make him brown as a berry and stimulate the growth of strong, straight bones and teeth.' "

"I've been meaning to get rid of those books," said Carly. "Look at all the space they take up."

Byrne smelled the musk of old knowledge, dead words, rising from the pages. As he returned the book to the shelf, he saw Carly in his periphery; she had come into the room, and was glowing with some quiet, shuddering anticipation.

She said, "So—what now?"

"I wouldn't mind a nap," Byrne said. "It was a long drive."

Carly smiled, trying feebly to overcome her disappointment. "It's three o'clock," she said. "How long do you want to nap?"

"I'm not sure." Byrne sat on the bed and began removing his workboots.

Carly took another step toward Byrne. Her hands were behind her back. "Can I get you anything?" she said. "An extra blanket?"

"No, thanks," said Byrne. He unbuttoned his plaid flannel shirt and took it off. "I guess I should have had a cup of coffee."

Carly blushed, averted her eyes. "I can make coffee here."

"Maybe later," Byrne said. He lay back on the pillow, his hands clasped on his chest.

Carly looked at him. "Kyle Byrne," she said. "That's a nice name."

Byrne closed his eyes. "It's the name my mother gave me," he said.

After a moment he heard Carly leave the room, and then there were noises of running water and clinking bottles. Within minutes he was dreaming.

—

Ted was on the sofa when the doorbell rang. He had fallen asleep there around four in the morning, drinking whiskey and listening to Sibelius's Fourth, and had not expected to be awakened anytime soon. Yet according to his watch it was ten in the morning. On a Sunday! No goddamned nigger of a Jehovah's Witness was worth the salt of his sleep. It was times like this that Ted wished he had a dog on the property. His last dog, Swinburne, had strangled himself in the curtains—Ted had come home one night to find him lying tangled like an angel engulfed in its own white wisps. That was two years ago. Now all Ted had was Kyle. And he was about to holler out for him—tell him to answer the bloody door—when he remembered that Kyle wasn't home, that he'd been gone since yesterday morning.

Ted swung his feet to the hardwood floor. He wore a pair of gray, tattered Jockey underpants and nothing else. He took a swig from the bottle of Jameson's on the low oak table, stood, and went to the front door, filled with atheist venom.

He looked through the peephole and was surprised to see the huge distorted face of a bald white man with the egg-shaped head and narrow eyes of a bull terrier. Swinburne had been part that. Curious, Ted chained the door and opened it an inch.

There were three men altogether. All of them wore suits.

Ted was mystified. "Hello?" he said.

"Kyle Byrne?" said the bald man. His tone was friendly and unassuming.

"No," said Ted, wondering if Kyle had entered a sweepstakes and won. Instantly Ted calculated that he was entitled to half.

"Are you Mr. Theodore Slocum?"

Ted squinted. Was it the IRS? He'd been meaning to get back to them.

"I'm Bill Messerschmidt," said the man. "FBI."

A badge was displayed.

"Could we ask you a few questions, Mr. Slocum?"

Ted ran his fingers over his ribs. The FBI?

"Kyle Byrne is a friend of yours, Mr. Slocum?"

"He's my brother," said Ted. He gripped the doorknob. "My half-brother. What's this about?"

"If you'll let us in, Mr. Slocum, we can go into more detail. It's a little chilly this morning."

Ted unfastened the chain, opened the door.

Messerschmidt looked him over. "We can wait a minute," he said, "if you want to get some pants on."

"I'd rather not," said Ted, feeling vaguely that there was some principle he was defending.

Messerschmidt shrugged, as if it were all the same to him. He introduced his associates as they gathered in the foyer, but Ted was thinking about the marijuana plants that he was cultivating in the basement closet.

"Mind if I sit down?" Messerschmidt said.

Ted hesitated. The presence of the men sensitized him to certain impurities in the room. It smelled of sweat and sleep and fried onions, with undertones of whiskey rising from his pores. He resented the conclusions that his visitors were probably drawing. He might explain to them that he, Ted Slocum, owned a vaunted secondhand bookstore in Fredericksburg, and that a collection of his poetry had been published fifteen years ago by a prestigious university press, not that these men would appreciate such things. Still, it comforted him, touching the dried-up leaves of those laurels. A man should never forget his accomplishments.

He led Messerschmidt to the sofa. The house was dark. There were leaning bookcases and dusty shelves buckling under the weight of old LPs. On the walls were some nude studies done by Ted, several framed photographs of his and Kyle's mother, a large red canvas with a black stripe supposedly painted by Ted's father (Ted had never met his father, just as Kyle had never met his), and, on the sliver of wall to the right of the window, a blowup of the cover of Ted's opus, *All That Moveth, Doth in Change Delight.* The floor-length curtains of the front windows were closed as a rule. Ted turned on the lamp beside the sofa, upon whose green corduroy cushions, faded and stained, Messerschmidt presently lowered himself. Ted cringed. It was *his* sofa, 'twas his bloody *bed,* he'd chewed those cushions in his sleep, had wrestled them, made love to them, made love *on* them, if memory served, and Swinburne, too, had been there, you could smell him deep in the material, the old grease and slobber, a scent like hickory smoke, that Messerschmidt was snuffing out. Ted was forced, then, to sit in the armchair, which faced the sofa. It was an antique, with palmette and cockleshell carvings. The cushion was rough and irritated his ass.

The other two men did not sit; one had positioned himself by the curtains, while the other, a tall black with wire-rim glasses, stood by the door. The black had a small circle of gray in his hair, as if lightning had touched it.

"Maybe you've heard, Mr. Slocum," Messerschmidt said, "about a shooting yesterday, at a family planning clinic."

Ted crossed his legs, which were thin and muscular, like a long-distance runner's. "An abortion clinic, you mean?" He reached for the pack of Winstons on the coffee table.

"Do you know where your brother is?" said Messerschmidt. "Because we'd like to ask him some questions."

"Why?" said Ted, lighting a cigarette. He held it between thumb and forefinger, like a straw. "Is he a suspect?"

"Would it surprise you?" said Messerschmidt.

Ted saw the man by the curtains pull them aside discreetly to peek out. He had the gold helmetlike hair of a news anchorman, and eyes that appeared widened by cosmetic surgery.

"No," Ted said. "I guess it wouldn't *surprise* me." He noticed that his ankle was twitching. "When you've got an open mind, nothing's too surprising." Ted cleared his throat, then descended into his cigarette; smoke rose from his head like the hair of a sinking man.

He loved his brother. He loved him, but he was also afraid of him. Their mother had taken some drugs during her pregnancy—a risky and complicated pregnancy at that; she was somewhere near forty—and it was Ted's judgment that poor Kyle had come out slightly damaged by it all. Mother and son, then, had nearly killed each other during those critical months; and it followed that in life they'd had an understanding, an empathy, from which Ted was hopelessly excluded. Mom would dote on Kyle like crazy, when she wasn't hacking out her lungs. When she finally died of emphysema—she'd been a heavy smoker most of her life—Kyle was only twelve, and Ted, at twenty-eight, was left in charge of the boy's upbringing. He hadn't published a poem since.

"What kind of car does he drive?" said Messerschmidt.

Ted squinted at the tip of his cigarette. "A blue one," he said. He glanced at the black man, who was still by the door, arms folded. His gold suit was too small for him, and had a sheen to it. Ted didn't own a suit.

"Where did he go?" said Messerschmidt.

Ted fidgeted. "Couldn't tell you," he said.

"This is a homicide, Mr. Slocum," said Messerschmidt. "You understand."

Ted nodded abstractedly. Then he reached for the bottle and drank. He didn't care to offer any to his guests. He set down the bottle and fell to looking at the twin skulls of his knees.

"As far as I know," he said, "he went to see a girl."

"Do you know her name?"

Ted shook his head.

Messerschmidt started jotting something on a pad.

"All I know," said Ted, feeling a little unnerved, "is that he met her on the Internet. One of those dating services. LoveSearch, I think it's called." Ted didn't add that he'd been corresponding with his own girl on LoveSearch. Her screen name was Femcaesura, and she lived in Richmond. Ted hadn't seen her picture—she hadn't posted one—but he'd been drawn by her stated tastes in literature, which reflected his own. They'd had some rousing exchanges on the topic. In his last e-mail, Ted had suggested that they meet for sex.

"Does he spend a lot of time on the computer?" said Messerschmidt, looking up.

Ted nodded. "It's his whole universe." He then felt compelled to add: "But he would never *kill* anybody. He isn't capable."

"Before you said you wouldn't be surprised."

"I said I wouldn't be surprised if he were a *suspect*." Ted recrossed his legs. "If you knew him, you'd understand what I mean."

"Apparently," said Messerschmidt, "an ex-girlfriend of his thinks he *is* capable. She contacted us when she heard about the incident; she told us he had a vendetta against the doctor who performed her abortion."

"She's a damn liar," Ted said, the fraternal knot tightening in his chest. "*She's* the one with the vendetta—against my brother. After she got that abortion, he left her."

Messerschmidt returned his pad to an inner pocket. "Would you mind," he said, "if I took a quick look at his room?"

Ted batted his eyes. Did they intend to search the house? He'd better play ball then. He stood and grumbled something about the Fourth Amendment, just loud enough to be heard.

He led Messerschmidt around a corner; the other men hung back.

As always, the door to Kyle's room was closed. Ted opened it, turned on the light. Messerschmidt entered and looked around thoughtfully, like a building inspector judging the structural integrity of the walls. The room was orderly and without any smell. Ted sensed that Messerschmidt approved of it as an oasis of sobriety.

"Is that your brother?" said Messerschmidt, nodding at the portrait that hung over the bed.

"Yes," said Ted. "I painted it."

"A striking young man."

"Perhaps what's striking," said Ted, "is the rendering." He saw that Messerschmidt was gazing at the portrait, as if bewitched.

"I'll bet he has lots of girlfriends," said Messerschmidt.

Ted grunted. "Not as many as you think."

Messerschmidt smirked. "Well," he said, "that's a goddamned relief." He laughed, and so did Ted. Ted had always been affected by the heartiness of big men. He wanted to have some drinks with Messerschmidt, and then try to pronounce his name. Just once, he would like to roll up his sleeves in a tavern with some men who carried guns. Ted had never even gone hunting—part of the privilege of having grown up fatherless.

"Are these him too?" said Messerschmidt, who was now inspecting the numerous framed photos on the dresser. "All of them?"

"Pretty much." Ted wondered if it was strange for a person to have so many pictures of himself on display. Like most babies, Kyle had been fascinated with his image—Ted reminisced to Messerschmidt how Kyle, as a toddler, used to sit for hours in front of the mirror on their mother's bedroom door, touching the glass.

Messerschmidt nodded thoughtfully. "That's how it is with little ones." He was silent for a moment, then said, "The ex-girlfriend seems to think he never outgrew that."

"How so?"

"She said he only loved himself."

Ted chuckled. "All that means," he said, "is that he didn't love *her.* She wasn't right for him anyhow. He met her online, of course. She was attractive, educated, career-minded. Kyle barely finished high school, and thinks he's an angel."

"So I heard." Messerschmidt picked up a recent picture of Kyle and looked carefully at it. "I'm surprised he'd have to go through the personals. Thought that stuff was for more awkward types. Like me, for instance."

"He's shy," said Ted. "He meets all his girls that way. It's easier for him."

"Shy?" Messerschmidt set down the picture. "Can't be too shy if he gets naked in front of strangers, now, can he?"

"He needs the money."

"I'll bet he wouldn't be shy if he met himself," said Messerschmidt.

"No," said Ted. "Probably not."

Messerschmidt's attention then fell on the computer that rested on the spotless desk.

"LoveSearch, you said the name was?"

"Why?" said Ted. "Are you looking too?"

"No, no, not me," said Messerschmidt, twisting the gold band on his ring finger. "I wouldn't know where to begin."

"It's easy," said Ted, with the enthusiasm of a hobbyist who senses interest in his collection. "You're either the hunter or the prey. You can look for women, or you can put your image out there, and have them look for you."

"Seems you'd have more of a pick if you were the hunter," said Messerschmidt, offhand, as if to hide his interest. "Otherwise, they'd have to find *you.*"

"In that case, you could just flood the system."

"What do you mean?"

Ted eyed his brother's portrait on the wall. "I mean, you could put your face in every city. Increase your odds. Imagine: the love of your life could be in Butte, Montana, or in New Orleans. Anywhere. Russia. India. Newport News." Ted laughed at the absurdity of it all.

So many possibilities, yet so much loneliness. He looked at Messerschmidt. "I've been writing to a woman," he said. "She lives right in Richmond. I've never been much of a traveler."

—

Byrne managed to survive the weekend without yielding to Carly's advances; on Saturday evening they had dinner at a place called the Carriage House, then went to the multiplex ten miles away. They saw a romance starring an actor whom Carly kept insisting Byrne resembled. Byrne watched impassively, more concerned about the perfumed hand that had landed on his knee. He covered it with his own, to make sure it traveled no higher. He was looking for nothing more than sanctuary.

They spent Sunday around the house. Carly had mentioned some yard work that needed to be done, and after a late breakfast at the kitchen table, Byrne, to earn his keep, went outside and took up the rake, then afterward got on a ladder and cleared the old dead leaves from the gutters while Carly ran some errands in town.

At one point, a young deer appeared on the edge of the woods, not fifty yards from the house: it stood there, looking at Byrne, suffused in the startling light of its perfection. Byrne froze on the ladder. After a moment, the deer turned and leapt away; its hooves made a wooden *pock* that echoed amid the trees.

That night, Carly appeared in Byrne's room in a sheer white negligee, and Byrne had to explain that he wanted to take things slowly, that he was an old-fashioned sort, and that if she could only be patient . . .

The speech seemed to work. When Carly left for work on Monday morning—she was a receptionist at a veterinary office—she was in good spirits, knowing, at the very least, that a man would be waiting there when she returned.

The day was warm and Byrne decided to take a walk, to find a pay phone; he was reluctant to drive, or to make any long-distance calls from Carly's house. Something told him to take extra care.

He walked for two miles, until he came across a gas station and a convenience store. There was a phone outside the store. Byrne called his brother at his bookshop.

"Paradise Lost," came Ted's voice.

Byrne listened as the operator asked Ted if he would accept the call. Ted did.

"Kyle," he said. "Jesus." His voice grew confidential. "Where are you?"

"Is something wrong?" Byrne said.

"Yes," said Ted. "Something is wrong."

Byrne listened to a story of how the cops had come and asked Ted questions about a murder, then left and came back with a search warrant, and seized Byrne's computer, as well as some photographs. Also—Ted was fairly certain—they had wiretapped their home phone.

Byrne was speechless; he could not understand how this had happened.

"Did you have anything to do with this?" Ted demanded.

"Of course not," said Byrne, but his voice quavered. "I don't know anything about it."

"It was your ex-girlfriend that tipped them off," said Ted, sounding unmoved by Byrne's denial. "Diane. Wasn't that her name? She heard about this doctor who was shot, and she thought you might have been involved, so she called the police."

Byrne was silent. *Diane.* He hadn't seen her in two years. After the abortion she'd moved to New Mexico, or one of those states. Byrne had not figured her in his calculations.

And yet *she* was the cause of all of this. When she first told Byrne that she was pregnant, Byrne had been overjoyed. He'd always wanted children. But Diane had other ideas. She wanted to travel, to study, to *live;* motherhood was something for later. *I'm only twenty-two.* Byrne could not understand it. There was a life inside her. A life! He begged her to reconsider. Genetically, it was as much *his* child as it was hers. It was a part of him, the very protein of his substance, an

Adam in his own image. Diane was eight weeks' pregnant on the day she went to the clinic. Byrne had already done some research and had discovered what an eight-week-old fetus looked like. He'd seen the feet and the hands, perfectly formed, and the head, unmistakably human; and no one could convince him afterward that it was not a life, and that to abort it was not murder. A spark had clicked, flown, caught; the miracle of creation had been kindled. To quench that light was an unholy act. And yet with a tube and suction, the deed had been done. Byrne had been haunted ever since. A possibility had been erased from history, forever; it was a loss that could not be measured. Byrne was not religious, but word of the pregnancy had given him a sudden knowledge of God. The ultimate force of the universe had spoken. More than once, Byrne had nearly convinced Diane to carry the baby to term; together they had imagined what the child would look like, act like, what its talents might be, they'd even considered names, *argued* about names. Kyle for a boy; Kelly or Kira for a girl.

By week eight, the skeleton had begun to harden; simple reflexes occurred, and the external sex organs could clearly be seen.

"Diane's just out to get me," Byrne said defiantly, "for leaving her."

"I told them that."

"You did?"

"Yes," said Ted.

"Thanks, brother." Byrne wondered what else Diane had told the cops.

"You know they got your password, too," said Ted.

"What?"

"Your password. When they took your computer, there was a little slip of paper underneath, with a word on it."

Byrne said nothing.

"They'll have access to all your files. I hope you didn't write anything incriminating."

"No," said Byrne. He felt sick. "I have to go now."

"Kyle!"

Byrne hung up the phone and set off toward the house. His first concern was that they'd read his correspondence with Carly. Included in those e-mails were directions to the diner where he and Carly had met. The cops would go there, then, and ask questions, pass around pictures. Maybe they were there right now. Byrne wondered if they could have gotten Carly's name and address from her Internet provider. Would her privacy be protected, even if she herself weren't a suspect? Byrne didn't think so. They might be waiting at Carly's this minute. If so, Byrne would cooperate. They could judge his innocence for themselves. Besides, they'd have a hundred other leads—surely they were looking into all the fanatics on the Internet who had posted threatening messages about abortionists. Why should they suspect only Byrne?

Approaching the house, Byrne saw through some trees that there were no additional cars in the driveway. He heard a whimper of relief jump from his throat.

He entered through the back door, with one of the keys that Carly had left for him. Georgie greeted him with loud barking. Byrne let him out into the yard. Then he went to his room and sat down at Carly's computer.

His hands were shaking as he logged on. He was curious to know if Carly had received any mail.

She had. It was from a WhiteKnight29. Byrne decided to open it.

To: GeorgieGirl
From: WhiteKnight29
    Hi GeorgieGirl, I noticed your personal ad and I think you are very beautiful and that we have a lot in common, everything in fact. I would like to tell you about myself and would like to know more about you. Please write as soon as possible. WK

Byrne stroked his whiskers. The words felt like a threat to his preeminence in the house. He dashed off a short response.

Hi WK. Thanks for writing, but I already met somebody. GG

Byrne then went into the website of the *Times-Dispatch* back home to see if there were any updates about the case. A headline read "Probe into Abortion Shooting Widens," but before Byrne could read the article, there appeared, in the upper left corner of the screen, a notice that he had received an instant message from WhiteKnight29.

Byrne flinched; the intrusion was like a hand slipping into his pocket.

He thought to ignore it, but the request shone there with such insistence that he felt compelled to accept.

WHITEKNIGHT29: Hi there.

Byrne tried to think of something.

GEORGIEGIRL: what do you want?
WHITEKNIGHT29: jeez don't be so mean, I'm a nice guy
GEORGIEGIRL: im sure
WHITEKNIGHT29: are you at work?
GEORGIEGIRL: maybe
GEORGIEGIRL: where are you?
WHITEKNIGHT29: not far from you.
WHITEKNIGHT29: Moller's Junction

Byrne hesitated. Moller's Junction? He'd never heard of it.

WHITEKNIGHT29: you familiar with it?

Byrne was afraid to respond; he felt like he was being tested.

GEORGIEGIRL: I told you I met somebody
WHITEKNIGHT29: met him? in person?
GEORGIEGIRL: maybe
WHITEKNIGHT29: how do you know you'd like him more than me?
GEORGIEGIRL: I like the way he looks

WHITEKNIGHT29: you haven't seen me yet
WHITEKNIGHT29: but I've seen you, Georgie
WHITEKNIGHT29: you're very pretty
GEORGIEGIRL: so what
WHITEKNIGHT29: so about this other guy. Have you met him?
GEORGIEGIRL: maybe
WHITEKNIGHT29: where's he from?

Byrne felt a buzz. It was the cops!

They had infiltrated, they were trying to get information. He knew this: he knew it in his blood.

His mind raced, trying to recall Carly's syntax, her style, her language. He remembered that she favored the exclamation point.

GEORGIEGIRL: none of your business!
WHITEKNIGHT29: come on, I want to know what sort of man I'm up against
GEORGIEGIRL: a better one than you!!!
WHITEKNIGHT29: you torture me
GEORGIEGIRL: okay I met him
WHITEKNIGHT29: you did?
GEORGIEGIRL: he came to visit!
WHITEKNIGHT29: is he still there?
GEORGIEGIRL: no he left yesterday :(
WHITEKNIGHT29: to visit another girl, I bet
GEORGIEGIRL: I doubt it!!
WHITEKNIGHT29: why, where did he say he was going?
GEORGIEGIRL: back home
WHITEKNIGHT29: where's that?
GEORGIEGIRL: Virginia!!
WHITEKNIGHT29: was it a nice visit?
GEORGIEGIRL: yes
GEORGIEGIRL: he's really nice!
GEORGIEGIRL: I have to go now!
WHITEKNIGHT29: maybe I can call you?

GEORGIEGIRL: no, sorry
GEORGIEGIRL: bye!

Byrne exited. His teeth were chattering. He wasn't sure what to do. If it really *was* the cops, maybe he had managed to throw them off the trail, for the time being. But he couldn't be sure. He was anxious to check his own e-mail, but knew that if he went online right now, under his own screen name, it would look strange, since whoever was tracking Carly's movements was no doubt tracking his. Byrne pictured someone in a crime lab, surrounded by computers, waiting for him to appear.

He decided to wait at least an hour before going back online.

He sat on the bed, his fist at his mouth. Things had become more complicated than he'd figured. He would need some help. He knew that if he seduced Carly, slept with her, she would do anything for him—she'd cover for him, defend him, at any cost. But he could not sleep with her. The shooting had changed him, had ruined him for mere mortals. He walked among the gods now, a nimbus of glory surrounded him, he knew, despite his nervousness. In a way it always had. When he was little, people compared him to an angel; his mother even told him that if he looked closely in the mirror he could see the scars where his wings had been clipped. Byrne did this, turning his head until his neck cramped up; and he thought he saw them, two faint marks on either shoulder blade. But he could never be entirely sure. For all the attention he devoted to the front of his body, there was still that region of himself that would always be a stranger to him, a long broad wall of flesh and bone that could never be feast for his senses. How he wished to be able to stroke his back from neck to tailbone, touch his lips to its salt skin, feel its knobs, its ribbing, observe its constellations! It was the vulnerable spot, the place of exposure. Byrne had not planned to shoot the doctor in the back, but it happened to be the target that presented itself, wide and faceless as he advanced to the doors of the clinic: Byrne fired two shots, made two tidy holes for where they could mount that murderer on two burning hooks in hell.

—

Ted set aside his reading of Donne's sonnets and went online. He typed in lovesearch.com. It was a recent diversion of his to search for love during store hours. Business was slow. He would be lucky to sell a single book today. Regardless, he could never resist acquiring more: novels, histories, biographies, poems, books on physics, on philosophy, on mathematics, on art, books on animals, on the cosmos, holy books, cookbooks, children's books, travel books, atlases, all brought to him several times a week in milk crates, shopping bags, and cardboard boxes. The walls were covered ceiling to floor with packed bookcases, and his desk was obscured under precarious towers of books waiting to be priced and shelved. These piles never seemed to dwindle. Sometimes Ted thought of his store as a kind of dumping ground for the printed word.

He got onto LoveSearch, but instead of punching in keywords such as *poetry* and *literature,* he decided, this time, to go strictly by looks. That meant he must disqualify any ad without a photo—a direct response to what had happened with Femcaesura. That little affair was over. Oh, it had been promising enough. She was thirty-six, childless, and a Ph.D. candidate in eighteenth-century British literature. Her grammar and spelling were immaculate. But Ted's curiosity got the better of him, and he'd asked her to send him a picture before they met, which went against his original conviction that he must strive at all costs for a pure spiritual union, a closeness unpolluted by baser considerations. As it happened, he received her e-mail the previous night, not long after Messerschmidt and company had left with various of Kyle's possessions. Shaken by the day's events, Ted had downloaded her photograph with wild hopes, only to find that she was not nearly as attractive as she'd claimed. In point of fact, she had the long, narrow head of an Afghan hound, and the same long, silky white hair that grows down from an Afghan's ears, framing its face, giving it a womanly aspect. Ted was crushed. Yes, language could be powerful and seductive; yes, one could fall in love with words, but the language of form, of symmetry, had a power all its own, and was still the chief tongue of Eros. The poets understood this; *they* seduced with words, but it was physical beauty that inspired those words, and feminine beauty in particular, the genius of Nature, the fire at which poets knelt; yes, Beauty was the true seducer, no Donne had ever required an unlaced mistress to turn a graceful phrase.

No wonder, then, that Kyle had done so well on the Internet. His image made words superfluous. One could draw him, paint him, but Ted had found it impossible to approach his corporeality through language. For his own part, Kyle could barely string together two sentences. He insulted language; he could capture a woman at will.

But now it was he who was about to be captured. Messerschmidt had seemed confident about that. "We'll find him," he'd said, when Ted had suggested, with some pride, that Kyle might outfox them all. But Ted believed in Messerschmidt. The FBI had manpower, hardware, science; Kyle had only his wits.

Maybe it would be better if Kyle *were* caught, Ted reasoned. If he *did* shoot that doctor—and Ted could not rule it out entirely—then who was to say that he wouldn't kill again?

Naturally, then, Ted wondered if there was something he could have done to avert this situation. But it was too late for that. The question was what to do *now.* He felt he'd handled things appropriately this morning, when Kyle had called; rather than lure him into the jaws of Messerschmidt, he'd warned him, clearly and fairly, that he was a hunted man. He'd given him a chance. What more ought one do for a killer?

Sitting alone amid his books, Ted feared that Kyle might try to come home.

———

Byrne went back online, this time under his own name. The icon of a yellow envelope appeared in the tiny mailbox: it was like an evil eye, watching him. Byrne drew a breath, then clicked on it.

The sender was "bjmess@fbi.gov."

Byrne stared. So here it was, he thought. The enemy had come.

Dear Mr. Byrne,

As you may have heard, I've been interested in chatting with you about a criminal investigation being conducted by my office. At present we are pursuing several leads in this case, and I'd like to ask you a few simple questions for the record. You may e-mail me, or call me at 804-261-1044. I appreciate your cooperation and look forward to hearing from you.

Yours truly,
Bill Messerschmidt

Byrne read the paragraph several times. It was obviously a trap. Did they think he was dumb? Did Ted tell them he was dumb?

It scared Byrne to think that they imagined such a ploy would work. That meant they were capable of anything.

Byrne wrote his response.

Mr. Messerschmidt, I don't know what you want with me but I am due to return home tomorrow and will call you then. KB

Byrne hoped that this would buy him time to think about his next move. The fear welled up in him and he considered turning himself in, reasoning that they had nothing on him, other than the accusations of a vindictive woman in New Mexico who could easily be discredited. But what if they had something else, Byrne thought; something he hadn't considered? A piece of surveillance tape, maybe? And what about those e-mails he'd exchanged with the gun dealer who'd sold him the Colt? It worried Byrne that he hadn't thought of these things before. What else hadn't he thought of?

He would have to keep moving, then. But where would he go? Should he just start driving? He'd already claimed that he would be back in Virginia tomorrow. That was one little decoy, which they probably weren't even buying. He ought to give them another. He should try to trick them, like the thief in a movie who stretches the resources of law enforcement by calling in a dozen bomb threats.

Byrne needn't go *that* far. All he had to do was strike up a dialogue with another woman, another Carly, and persuade her to let him come visit. The FBI, monitoring his e-mails, would then dispatch agents to the point of rendezvous. Byrne imagined a football field, on which the opposition was drawn all to one side, leaving huge daylight on the other.

He entered LoveSearch.

His first step was to select the city or state that he wanted to explore. Studying the map, Byrne eyed the northeast; if he drew his pursuers to that corner, with others waiting in Virginia, he could head due west, into cornfields, with the plains beyond. Somewhere in America, he would disappear.

Once you chose a locale on LoveSearch, you were then presented with a long list of come-ons ("Lover wanted," "Hot chick seeking nice guy" "RU4 me?"), and when you found one that grabbed you, you clicked on it, and a photo and biography followed. Byrne had clicked on the city of Boston, and was baffled to find such puzzling hooks as "Isolde seeks a Tristan" and "Svelte empiricist wants hard evidence." One phrase did intrigue him, however. It read, "Don't Burn. Be Reborn." Byrne stared at those words, feeling for some reason that they referred to him specifically, even though he didn't think he had anything for which to repent. It was like a provocation. Burn? Him? Why should *he* burn? What about the doctor? What about all the doctors?

Annoyed, he downloaded the photo, not knowing what to expect. But when the picture appeared, Byrne put his hand to his throat.

It was the strangest, most fascinating face he'd ever seen. A beautiful face, slightly masculine, hinting at a chic androgyny; a familiar face, a face from his dreams, as of a lover, a kindred spirit. He understood this person, he felt. He wanted her. He knew this instantly. He rarely wanted anyone, but when he did, it became a fixed idea and he pursued it to the end. He stared at the face so intently that the eyes appeared to move; and it was then that he realized there was something wrong with her. Her beauty appeared unnatural, as if she were disfigured once, and her face remade by wizards. *Don't Burn.* Byrne considered that phrase. Had there been an actual fire? Byrne saw no scars, but the image could have been enhanced, altered. Or perhaps she did mean it in a biblical sense—as an appeal to a sinner—and it was the power of the Infinite within her that graced her outward appearance. She had black hair to her shoulders, blue eyes as bright as cut sapphires, an aristocratic nose, and a wide, shapely mouth that seemed to be suppressing, in its perfect neutrality, a pair of fangs and a forked tongue. That, or she was a true angel of heaven: she was nothing in between. Her age was hard to determine—she seemed not so much young as ageless—and she had chosen not to tell. Her handle was Nemesis2001 (whose nemesis? God's or the Devil's?), and her statement was brief: *Surrender to me, and I'll take you to Heaven. Together we can escape this fallen world, together we can make angels, and they will inherit the Earth. (Please send a picture.)*

Byrne was ecstatic. He rushed to send her his photograph, along with a note saying that he needed to meet her immediately, and to give him her phone number—he would call her from somewhere on the road, they could make their arrangements on the fly. Byrne could see no other way.

He brought her image back to the screen and looked into the eyes. His hands were clasped tightly together.

Here she was, he thought—his reward, for having avenged the innocent. Byrne had never been in love before, but he had dreamed of love, and it had felt like this.

He leaned forward and kissed the lips on the screen.

He then heard a noise from the living room—the front door. Georgie barked from outside. Byrne's trance was shattered.

Who was it?

He went to the window, prepared to lift it so that he could dive out. The sky was purple and orange, the trees black. He could run into the woods.

"Kyle?" came a voice. "Yoo-hoo!"

It was Carly.

Byrne exhaled, wiped his hands on his shirt. "I'm in here," he said.

Carly approached timidly—Byrne discerned this in the sound of her steps—then stopped in the doorway and poked in her head.

"I tried calling," she said, "but the line's been busy forever." Her cheerfulness betrayed her suspicion. "Were you online?"

"A little," said Byrne. "I was listening to music. Downloading some old songs."

"Which songs?" said Carly, her interest exaggerated by her desire to believe him.

"All kinds," said Byrne. "What'd you do today?"

Carly laughed. "What do you think? Somebody brought a pet pig in. It had depression."

"Maybe it just needs some mud," said Byrne. He then noticed the car keys dangling on Carly's finger.

He thought: the car. *Her* car. Pennsylvania tags.

He could take her car. He could drive her car to Boston.

"Well, let me get out of these clothes," Carly said. "Are you hungry?"

"A little."

"Good. I'll be quick." Carly disappeared.

Byrne stood there. He could drive to Boston in the hatchback, undetected. Once there, he could go to a library, or an Internet café, and send an e-mail to Nemesis2001, telling her that he was in Pennsylvania, and would be in Boston in a couple of days. In reality, he'd be able to reach her in minutes, well before the cops made their move.

From the bathroom Byrne heard a rush of water.

He wondered if he should just take the car now. But no: Carly would report it stolen, and he'd be worse off than he would in his own car. He'd have to ask to borrow it. But how? On what pretext?

Byrne paced the room. He heard the screech of the faucets as the water was shut off. A moment later, the bathroom door opened. Was she coming this way? Byrne looked around. He saw the ceramic dog on the dresser; without thinking he picked it up. It was cold and heavy.

"Kyle?" Carly was standing by the doorway, just out of view.

Byrne froze. "Huh?"

"Will you put some lotion on my back?"

Byrne said nothing.

Carly then appeared, wearing only a large yellow bath towel; her skin was pink, flushed from her bath and a certain tingling excitement that caused her to take one tentative step into the room.

Byrne kept the statue behind him, gripping it in one hand. He had no idea what he was doing.

"Who's *that*?" Carly said, her eyes fixed sharply on the computer screen. She advanced to get a closer look, moving past Byrne, who stood there helplessly.

"Don't!" Byrne said, and without thinking he lunged and brought the statue down upon the back of her skull, striking her with such force that he could feel, through his hand and up his arm, the bolt of life that must have instantly left her: the next thing Byrne knew she was crumpled on the floor in front of the desk. Everything was silent.

Byrne dropped the statue and went to Carly's bedroom. It contained a bed, a television, two old wooden dressers, and a vanity in whose mirror Byrne saw his pale, unshaven face: in the dim light he looked as scared and incongruous as a deer that had just slammed through a window.

He turned and saw the car keys on the flowered bedspread. Beside them was Carly's black handbag. Byrne pocketed the keys, then turned the bag upside down. Among the items that fell out of it was a wallet. Byrne opened the wallet, took out all the bills, and pocketed them, too. Then he returned to the other room.

The body hadn't moved. Byrne did not know if he was appalled or relieved. He went to the desk and switched on the color printer. Because of the body he had to lean over the desk at an awkward angle. Carly's towel was still fastened, but the cups of her buttocks were exposed. Byrne printed out the photograph of Nemesis2001. He watched as the image was rolled out to his fingertips, the face even more alive to him on the paper than it had been on the screen. Now he could hold it in his hands.

He heard a groan.

He looked down. Carly's hand had traveled to the back of her head.

Byrne felt a panic. Should he run? But no—he couldn't just leave her like this. He crouched and spoke in her ear.

"Are you okay?" he said.

"Daddy."

Byrne was silent.

"It hurts," said Carly. Her voice was barely audible.

Tenatively, Byrne touched her hair.

He said, "Do you know Kyle?"

"Kyle."

"Yes. The man who came to see you. Do you remember him?"

There was no answer. Byrne moved the hair from over her ear, and saw that the ear was plugged with a thick clot of blood. Byrne jumped up.

He was aware of his own breathing as he packed his bag. He went out and closed the door behind him. Georgie was still barking outside.

Byrne went to the kitchen and opened the back door. Georgie came in, hungry. Byrne filled the bowl to overflowing, and left the bag out so that Georgie could get to it if he had to. He also changed Georgie's water, filling the dish to the rim. Some of the water spilled over as he slowly set it down.

He left the back door open, so that Georgie could get out.

—

The hatchback had a full tank of gas—enough to get to Boston, Byrne calculated. He retrieved some maps from the glove compartment of his own car. He wasn't sure how long it would take him to get to Boston, but it was dark now and it would surely be dark when he got there—he'd have to wait out the early morning hours in the car, on a side street, until he could get to someplace that had a computer. With any luck, Nemesis2001 would have replied to his e-mail by then, and given him her phone number. Byrne would then call her and arrange to meet.

Byrne drove onto the highway where the diner was and headed north to the interstate. All he needed was to make it to Boston. The map was folded on the dash, and on the seat next to him was the picture of Nemesis2001: Byrne could not keep himself from glancing at it.

Each pair of headlights in the rearview was like a threat on his life.

Byrne turned on the radio and found a station playing classical music, which reminded him of his brother. He wondered if Ted had believed him today, on the phone. Probably not. Ted had always been wary of him, Byrne felt.

Byrne kept catching his own eyes in the mirror, and sometimes this would distract him from his thoughts; or else the beams coming toward him in the opposite lane lashed his face, and left, as they fled, a ghost of his own image in the side window, an image that persisted if he concentrated on it, hanging there in the glass, to be washed away again by another blast of light.

He took the picture of Nemesis2001 in his right hand and held it so that it would be illuminated in the oncoming beams. It was the one face that could beguile him as much as his own; in fact there was even a kind of resemblance, Byrne saw—he hadn't really noticed it before. The eyes, he thought. He looked more closely, then checked his own eyes in the mirror. Yes, the eyes: and the mouth, too—it was almost the same exact mouth. Anxious, Byrne held the picture beside the mirror. He looked between both, and then he realized where he'd seen the face before: it looked like a picture of him that he kept on his desk at home, taken last year—but before he could make any further connection, he heard the blaring pitch of a car horn. He then saw his own frozen expression in the side window—there was a screech of tires, a panel of black night, and a sudden, hovering mass—and in a clash of steel his head flew into the windshield, which caught him, held him, in its crystal web.

—

Ted had decided to look for a new puppy online, but each dog that came up on the screen had a curiosity in its eyes, a kind of dreamy, unformed intelligence that reminded him unpleasantly of Kyle. He pondered getting a cat instead. He needed company. The house had become strangely quiet without Kyle; there was a sense of some living thing holding its breath behind doors, waiting crouched around corners. Ted didn't believe in ghosts, but having more or less reared his brother it was only natural that he'd feel a pang of responsibility for what had become of him, even though he knew it was all decided beforehand, that destiny had been written in the womb. Three people were dead. Kyle would have said that it was four.

Ted had yet to unpack the box of Kyle's things—his computer and the pictures from his desk—that had been returned to him from Messerschmidt's office just before Christmas. The package came to the bookshop and was promptly shoved by Ted into a corner behind the register, and was now covered with stacks of old, mildewy books. Ted was never sure why the authorities had confiscated the pictures—they must have put them on TV, or on the Internet, under "Most Wanted." Kyle hadn't given them a chance. He'd driven off the road and into a tree; an apparent suicide. Ted had never claimed to understand his brother.

In any case, Ted found himself spending more and more time at the shop, staying deep into the night, writing florid prose to various women on the Internet. He had so much to tell them.

Sometimes, when he found a face he really liked, he composed a poem and sent it off, not really caring if he got a response. It felt good simply to know that his words were being read. In the past two months he'd written more verse than he had in years. He'd even established contact with a couple of young lovelies, one in Sweden, another in Belgium. Why limit himself to a fifty-mile radius? If need be, he could sell the house and move anywhere. He felt lighter, freer. The heft of words, dusty and mite-ridden and in piles all around him, had achieved a new fluidity in his blood, gone from the hulk and mess of printed paper to the weightlessness of light traveling through space.

Late into the night, he zapped his love across oceans.

THE RISK-REWARD RATIO

Robert Anthony Siegel

Danny Price lived on a houseboat on the Gowanus Canal. Whenever anybody asked, he told them he loved it there—which had been true for the first couple of months, when it was all new and exciting. The canal and its environs made up a fascinating postindustrial ecosystem compounded of abandoned factories, rotting docks, floating tires, and sunken barges. After decades of industrial dumping, the water was a luminous green, the color of Scope. The smell was beyond chemical, however—reaching toward something dark and organic, reminiscent of death, decay, and bodily shame. The dogs that scavenged the wharves all seemed to be missing an eye or an ear, and the cats had no tails. The people looked worse and were more dangerous.

Danny had come with the intention of changing all that. He wasn't an environmentalist but an entrepreneur, what he liked to call a "guerrilla capitalist," by which he meant that he was in business for the adventure as much as the money. When he heard that the city was auctioning off an abandoned factory site by the canal, he was intrigued, and when he learned that there were plans to install a new lock on the canal, one that would flush the toxic water out to sea, he decided to bid. His idea was to knock down the factory and build a luxury marina.

Improbable, yes, but think of the possibilities: the only marina in South Brooklyn, just minutes from Wall Street by way of the tunnel. Where those sunken barges now lay, there would be a row of sleek yachts, flags fluttering in a sweet-smelling breeze. Where that wall of rusting oil drums stood, a ferry slip for the hovercraft to Manhattan. Waterfront condos would take the place of the factory building. The clubhouse would hold a four-star restaurant, with a terrace overlooking the canal. A helipad would go way out over there, near the lock, where the diesel pumps now stood. And there, that patch of broken glass where the wild dogs liked to fornicate—that would be the gazebo where the band played on summer nights, in a little park strung with Chinese lanterns. Couples would dance in the moonlight.

The city commission had loved it. His visionary presentation, combined with the absence of competing bids, had gotten him the factory. He was so stunned by his good fortune that he had stumbled out of the Municipal Building and wandered into the first bar he found in Chinatown, where he had spent the rest of the afternoon getting very drunk on something sweet that came in a ceramic skull, while the karaoke system played "Come Ye Back to Mandalay" over and over again.

Winning had cost him the four buildings he owned in Boerum Hill and the condo in Brooklyn Heights—all gone to buy the factory site. It had cost him his chance to buy a franchise in the Women's Professional Football League, an opportunity with enormous upside potential. Most important, it had also cost him his live-in girlfriend, Clarissa Wyre, who refused to move with him to the houseboat. This last was a source of continuing pain.

Danny was ready to concede that Clarissa had some grounds for complaint. The interior of the houseboat was spartan. The kitchen consisted of a hot plate, the rest of little more than a camp chair, folding table, and narrow bunk. The walls were damp and the floor often wet—he had never seen such a fascinating variety of molds. His books were all moldy. Even his clothes had mold growing on them now.

But that wasn't really the issue, as he had pointed out that night in Brooklyn Heights, when she left him.

"Of course it's not the issue," she had shouted back. "What do you think I've been telling you for the last three hours?"

He wasn't really sure, because for Danny, as soon as an argument began, it was like somebody had turned the sound off on the TV. Clarissa was still there, frowning, gesticulating, very rapidly moving her lips, but the words were all gone, and he had to try to make sense of the pictures: *She's pointing to something. She seems upset. She's clutching her head.*

But on that night Clarissa had disappeared into the bedroom, only to reemerge carrying a suitcase. "Hey, wait a second," he said.

"The *issue,* Danny, is that we are going nowhere. Because *you* are going nowhere."

He could only assume she was questioning his instincts about the marina. "This is a major opportunity, Clarissa. A onetime deal."

"I want to have a family."

He had a moment of fright while searching for the right answer. "*You're* my family."

"I want children. I want a home."

"We'll get there," he said, as if this were someplace far, far off, and almost impossible to find.

"No, we won't get there. *You* won't. But *I* will." And with that she had lifted her suitcase and headed for the door.

There had followed one of those agonized, impossible-to-define, neither-nor periods that can only be alluded to as *pre-postbreakup:* e-mails three or four times a day, with one side or the other threatening to change his or her e-mail address. Phone calls at two in the morning, full of demands that the other side stop calling. Meetings with more conditions attached than a Middle East summit, the point of which was to establish that there would be no more meetings under any conditions whatsoever—followed by frantic, shamefaced sex and then a week of silence, during which time each would be haunted by the fear that the other had been killed in a traffic accident.

It had gone around and around like that with no end in sight—one month, two—even as Danny sold his buildings and his condo, liquidated his stock portfolio, and moved into the houseboat. It had continued while he consulted with architects, engineers, and urban planners, while he talked to banks and contractors, while he used the last of his cash to install a security fence around the factory site.

And then suddenly it had stopped. "Don't call here anymore, Danny," Clarissa had said to him one night, after an unusually long period out of touch.

"That's *why* I'm calling," he told her. "We can't keep going around like this." Stretched out on his bunk, the cell phone to his ear, he had taken in the interior of the cabin with some satisfaction: blueprints spread over the folding table, correspondence stacked on the camp chair. The houseboat had actually seemed like an exciting place, back then—moldy, but exciting. "I've got too much on my plate right now to deal with your separation anxieties."

"Good, I'm glad you feel that way. So let's say goodbye and get it over with."

He was a little taken aback. These conversations usually went on for hours, while the wild dogs howled on the docks outside. They were an essential part of his bedtime ritual. "Well, okay, then. Sure. Let's do that."

"Goodbye, Danny. Don't get eaten."

"I'll invite you to the ribbon-cutting."

There was a pause. "No, I don't think so."

I don't think so. He gave her a week, then two, but to his great surprise she kept her word and didn't call. She didn't answer his phone messages, either, or his e-mails. And then, after he had sent a particularly exasperated little missive beginning WHAT'S A MAN GOTTA DO THESE DAYS TO GET SOME CLOSURE?, his e-mails started bouncing back undelivered. She had changed her e-mail address.

Nevertheless, he refused to accept the possibility that the relationship was not merely ending but truly *ended* until a conversation with a mutual friend by the name of Vikram Saraswathy. A devoted gossip, Saraswathy had been an excellent back-channel source of information about Clarissa ever since the breakup had begun, almost six months earlier. On this particular occasion, however, Danny had called not because of Clarissa, but because Saraswathy was a civil engineer, and there seemed to be some trouble with the new lock the city had installed on the canal. "It's not flushing," said Danny. "The water isn't moving."

"What happens?" asked Saraswathy.

"It just sits there, bubbling."

As luck would have it, Danny happened to be seated in an inch of the stuff at that very moment, the phone pincered between ear and shoulder while he struggled to disassemble a clogged bilge pump on the floor of the boat.

"Did they say what the problem with the lock was?" asked Saraswathy.

"Something about the tides and currents. I was hoping you could tell me."

"Hey, I do bridges. Canals are a whole different thing."

"If they can't get that lock working, I'm fucked," said Danny. He poked a screwdriver into the black sludge at the bottom of the valve. "Do you know something about bilge pumps at least? I think I've got a seepage problem here on the boat."

"Leakage?" asked Saraswathy, sounding alarmed.

"Seepage." This was an important distinction for Danny: leakage was bad; seepage was okay as long as the pumps worked.

"Don't know much about seepage, I'm afraid."

"Then I assume you haven't heard anything from Clarissa, either."

But Saraswathy *had* heard from her, just the other night, as it turned out. Clarissa, he told Danny, had started dating again—*cyber*dating.

Danny felt a distinct pressure rising in his chest, and his laughter was forced. "What, a chat room?" he crowed. "You know, I feel sorry for her, I really do."

"Not a chat room, a dating service."

"Poor woman."

"She says she's getting a lot of hits."

Hits. It flashed across Danny's mental landscape like a comet that these *hits* were men. "Women have no feelings."

It took him most of the night to get the pump working and the water out of the cabin, and when he came on deck for air it was light out—a weak, acidic white light that stung his eyes. The wildlife— human and otherwise—had all gone to burrow by then, and the wharves were empty of movement except for a single plastic bag driven around and around by the wind. Pre-postbreakup had had its charms; it was ugly and circular and exhausting, but it was also in- teresting, even exciting. It was a transitional phase, and thus offered all the fun of travel without the bother of actually leaving and going somewhere. He didn't have to miss Clarissa because he spoke to her all the time.

But *post*breakup was the real thing; it was arrival, and suddenly Danny didn't like where he had arrived: the splintered docks; the stretch of cracked paving littered with broken glass; the trash piled against the security fence; the windowless factory building he couldn't afford to pull down; the new canal lock that didn't work. *Post* was the blue car seat the winos had set in the tall weeds, sur- rounded by empty liquor bottles and Chinese takeout containers. *Post* was the trashcan fire slowly burning itself out, cinders spiraling upward. *Post* was the used condoms that littered the ground, and the rainbow sheen of oil that rode the surface of the canal, and the smell of diesel fuel when the wind shifted north, and the *whoosh-whoosh* of early morning traffic on the Gowanus Expressway off to the right, suspended high above the empty streets.

If they didn't get that lock working, *post* might well be forever.

Sleep was out of the question. He went inside, booted up his lap- top, located the dating service Saraswathy had mentioned—Seri- ousingles.com—and found Clarissa's page. But before he had a chance to read the essay she had posted there, the photograph stopped him cold. It was familiar, *very* familiar: not only had it been taken on a vacation he remembered all too well—on the beach in Hawaii—but he had once been the other half. She had cut him out.

—

He had been cut out, he had been made invisible, and like all invisible people, he knew deep in his bones that only the cruelest, bloodiest revenge would make him visible again. He fought against this knowledge, reminding himself how wasteful vengeance is, how it inevitably ricochets back on the vengeful, but all his philosophizing was to no avail. When you decide on revenge, the old saying goes, dig two graves. *How convenient,* thought Danny, looking around the cabin, *I'm already living in one.*

It was not until late that afternoon, however, lying in his bunk and listening to the back-and-forth creak of the hawsers, that he realized he had the perfect plan of action for an invisible man. He would visit Clarissa's dating page again, and this time he would read her little essay—no, not simply read, but study, analyze, *memorize,* until he knew her male ideal by heart. And then he would become that ideal. He would invent a new name and a new life, and disguised like that would correspond with her until she believed that the absurd fantasy man he had created to her specs was not only real but wonderful, kind, loving, and *good*—for *good,* spoken with extreme emphasis while crinkling up her eyes, was Clarissa's highest praise for people. Indeed, when the word *good* finally appeared in one of her e-mails, Danny would know that the time had come: he would suggest that they meet for dinner. You can guess the rest: Mr. Perfection would not show up for that dinner, but Danny Price would, and with a stunning new woman on his arm (even if he had to hire her, which seemed likely). As luck and a big tip would have it, they would be seated at the table next to Clarissa's.

This might not seem like much as revenge goes, especially compared to what people do to each other in places such as Sierre Leone or the Balkans. But it gave Danny great pleasure to imagine that dinner. My God, Clarissa, is that you? he would ask, and then give a completely unembarrassed laugh, meaning *I'm okay with this, to-*

tally okay, because I've moved on in my life. Oh, yes, I'm sorry, let me introduce you to Consuela/Tiffany/Saffron/Ming. We're engaged! I can hardly believe it myself, everything happened so fast! Saffron, show her the ring (gigantic, rented). He would catch Clarissa's eye for a moment, and then slowly look her up and down in a way that would both note and forgive each wrinkle and sag. We had some good times, though, didn't we, Clarissa? he would say. Thank God everything turned out for the best. And then he would glance at the two place settings on her table, and ask in his sweetest voice: Dining alone?

Danny could have stayed in bed the rest of the day, tweaking the details of this scene, dwelling on the way Clarissa stared at Consuela, her pained smile when she saw the ring, her choked congratulations—but there was far too much to do. By the end of business hours he had gotten a new e-mail address and membership in Seriousingles, and by dinnertime he had downloaded her page and printed out her essay. After a cold can of franks and beans—the hot plate had gotten soaked in the flood—he started giving her male ideal the kind of attention he normally reserved for contracts and blueprints.

The experience was shocking. Clarissa's essay opened with a preamble about love, trust, honesty, and commitment, then segued into a lengthy discourse on the need for roots. There was an almost mystical paragraph on something called "a sense of what's really important in life," which seemed to connect back to a short reminiscence about Thanksgiving and her grandmother's pumpkin pie. There was a paragraph about living in harmony with nature, and another about love of the simple pleasures. Sunsets were mentioned in this last category, as were falling leaves, the smell of coffee in the morning, trick or treat, yard sales, the Sunday *Times,* and driving in the rain. The clause about motherhood and children came near the end, but from the wording it seemed to be a deal breaker.

Danny found a damp, pulpy notebook and began scribbling

notes, trying to make sense of what he had just read. The nostalgia for country life was puzzling in a woman who grew up in Detroit and lived in Brooklyn, but so was the worship of simplicity. Clarissa worked in PR. Her glasses were large and rectangular. She chain-smoked Marlboro Lights and ate salad with her fingers while standing at the kitchen sink—that was her idea of dinner. She carried not one but *two* cell phones at all times.

Danny was tempted to dismiss the essay as an escapist fantasy, not to be taken seriously. What kept him working, however, as night deepened and the alley cats yowled outside, was the part at the very end about "a truly uninhibited man, unafraid of his own sensual nature." As he read this, steel bands seemed to wrap themselves around his head, ratcheting tighter, tighter, tighter, each time he took a breath. *There will be none of that,* he growled. *No blindfolds, no incense, no bong hits, no feather boa, and no strawberry love oil.*

By midnight, his own page was up.

Angus Green, Danny's fictive creation, was a potter who lived in a converted barn in Vermont. Much more important, he was a carefully crafted amalgam of every quality Clarissa claimed to value most in a man—what Danny listed in his notebook as the Four S's: Serious, Sensitive, Sensuous, and Centered. Angus grew organic vegetables in his garden. He taught yoga part-time in town. His house smelled wonderfully of wood smoke. He had bunches of rosemary drying in a basket in his kitchen, bottles of olive oil lined up on the counter. He had Whitman and Lao-tzu on the nightstand in his bedroom. He worried about nuclear proliferation and global warming. He baked his own bread. He wrote poetry. He was skilled at massage. Danny despised him.

And so, sitting on his bunk with his laptop on his knees, Danny began to type out his first message:

Dear Clarissa,
    I came across your page and had to tell you how deeply moved I was. I, too, have had the kind of reawakening you mention.

Good, thought Danny, stopping to read the line over. I can see him there, typing very earnestly at a rolltop desk: denim work shirt, ponytail, beard. Large hands, square shoulders, sensitive face. Mug of herbal tea.

As I write this, I look out my bedroom window into my meadow and my apple orchard. But just seven years ago I was a stockbroker in New York, and the view from my window was an airshaft. At night I fell asleep to CNBC, and the first thing I did when I opened my eyes in the morning was switch to *Market Watch*. All I cared about was the direction of the market, the cut of my suit, and the trajectory of my career.

Yes, he's been there, he knows where she's coming from!

It's not that I was shallow and vain, Clarissa—though I was those things—it was that I was so unhappy. If you're interested, I can tell you more about how I got back in touch with myself. The point I want to make here is that you shouldn't give up. The kind of life you are looking for is out there, and so is the right kind of guy.

Meaning, not the poor trusting fool you were with for almost five years, the one you left to rot on a toxic canal.

I am a potter now. There is no greater feeling than being up to your elbows in clay, making something beautiful that is also useful.

As opposed to selling everything you own in order to clean up urban blight, stimulate the local economy, and improve the city in which you live.

When I am working on the wheel, I feel that I understand my place in the world, and my reason for being. I am at the center of my universe, totally at peace.

Do you even say "working on the wheel"? Well, she won't know, either.

And yes, I have learned to take pleasure in the little things: chopping wood, pressing my own apple cider, skating on the pond in winter, cooking. Believe me, there is nothing like the smell of baking bread filling the house on a bright Sunday morning, as the light streams in the kitchen window. I like to take a couple of fresh loaves to my neighbors down the road. Neighborhood—a sense of community—is everything here.

Danny was interrupted just then by a familiar scratching at the hatch—river rats, trying to get in. They swarmed over the deck at night, chewing on whatever they could find. He had once made the mistake of going outside with a broom to shoo them away and had come back with a gnawed stick and a new sense of humility. He was now careful to lock himself in before dark, stuffing rags—which the rats pulled out and ate—under the door. He checked the .22 beside his bunk and went back to typing.

A family of rabbits just passed by my door—I wish you could have seen. We have deer, elk, and moose, too. Nature has restored me to myself, Clarissa. The birch woods are my church, and the long walks I take in them a form of prayer. You can see the face of God in a fallen leaf, in the sunset, in the flight of the sparrow,   .
in the laughter of children.

Risky, starting in on religion, but Danny judged this safely ecumenical stuff, indicative of a general spirituality, and the line about children was good. Besides, Clarissa had no religion at all and would be impressed.

I was particularly touched by the things you wrote about family. I have six brothers and sisters, and I know how rooted a big family makes you feel. I want that in my life.

Perfect: Clarissa was an only child. Danny typed a little more about centeredness and a sense of values, appended the name Angus Green, and clicked the SEND button.

—

Revenge seemed to be good for Danny. He slept deeply and woke suffused with a feeling of peace and possibility. It had occurred to him while still semiconscious that the problems with the lock could be traced back to Clarissa—that his entanglement with her had been holding the marina project back in some indefinable way. If he could only inflict full punishment on her—crush and humiliate her, as she had crushed and humiliated him—he would be able to move on. The lock would start working, financing would come through, the bilge pumps on the houseboat would keep pumping, and his jeans would finally dry. It was a happy thought.

He decided to celebrate this insight with breakfast al fresco—coffee and a roll on deck. This had to be done with great caution, however, because of the seagulls. The seagulls that prowled the canal were different from their brethren elsewhere, in much the same way that the dogs, cats, and rats were different—tougher, mostly, and with a taste for gratuitous cruelty. He had been attacked once in the early days, over a *paper napkin,* and still bore the scar on his hand. So he ate quickly now, hunkered low in an aluminum deckchair, his eyes scanning the sky. For that reason he didn't see the little boy walking up the gangplank.

"What you looking for?" asked the boy, following his gaze.

"Jesus, don't you knock?" asked Danny. He had been startled.

The boy looked around the deck skeptically. "Where?" He was eight or nine, probably, on the runty side, and extremely dirty.

"Who are you, anyway?" asked Danny.

"Carlos."

"Carlos, does your mother know you're here?"

That was the signal: Carlos began poking around the deck with great interest, as if he had missed the question. He yanked on a bumper, stepped on one of the hawsers, pressed his face to a porthole. Danny watched, sipping the last of his coffee. The boy was in jeans and a turtleneck, but there was something of the ancient nomad about him. Maybe it was the equipment he carried: a long stick in one hand, some kind of slingshot in his back pocket, a GI Joe without arms tucked upside down in his belt like a prisoner. He seemed to have everything he needed.

"You live here?" asked Carlos.

"I do."

"My sister says you're crazy."

"I'm an investor. It's not the same thing."

"Aren't you afraid of the dogs?"

"Aren't *you*?"

Danny looked at the boy, and the boy looked at Danny, and in that instant they read the truth in each other's face: Yes, they were afraid of the dogs. No, it didn't matter.

"There's treasure in there," said Carlos, by way of explanation, and then gestured toward the old factory—Danny's factory.

Finally, thought Danny, *somebody with brains.* He got up from his chair and wiped the crumbs from his lap, giving the sky one last scan for incoming gulls. "Carlos, do you want a soda before you go home?"

Down in the cabin, the boy went through much the same routine as up top, touching everything, turning on and off whatever appliances still worked. Within minutes, his dark palm prints were everywhere, even the ceiling. Nevertheless, he managed to work his way through two bottles of Coke, a Slim Jim, and a bowl of Froot Loops. While Carlos ate his cereal, Danny unfurled the blueprints for the marina and showed him what he was planning: the docks, the condos, the little park with the gazebo and the Chinese lanterns. The boy's eyes took it all in. His questions were sharp—how many apartments, how many boats? How would people get there? Danny showed him the garage and the ferry slip. Carlos nodded, crunching Froot Loops. "What you need," he said, "is a place for the helicopters."

Danny's eyes narrowed. "Why is that?"

"In the future everybody will go by helicopter."

And so Danny showed him the helipad he had placed out by the lock. "You have a feeling for this, Carlos. There are men five times your age who don't get it. My own girlfriend doesn't get it." *Didn't get it,* he corrected himself mentally. *Past tense.*

But the boy was preoccupied with calculations of his own. "What about the treasure?" he asked. With a dirty finger, he began tracing the outline of the condos on the blueprint—the space where the factory building now stood.

"You mean the rate of return?" Excellent question—the kid really was sharp! Danny began searching through the stack of papers on the camp chair, looking for a copy of his business plan. "I've got some projections right here."

"No, the *treasure,*" said Carlos. "In the factory."

"Oh, *that* treasure." Danny put down the papers and looked at the boy more closely. Carlos had big brown eyes, and curly hair in a wild tangle. It dawned on him that this strange nomad was—he had to struggle with the idea—not exactly like himself. Not a miniaturized adult, but not a happy-go-lucky kid, either. A pair of plastic sunglasses atop Carlos's head gave him a strangely jaunty air, as if he'd just jumped out of a convertible, but his face looked worried in a way that had nothing to do with play or make-believe. "If the treasure's there, it's yours," said Danny. "That's our deal."

Danny understood that look better when he walked the boy home. Carlos lived with his sister in one of the tenements on the other side of the highway—buildings so old the brick facades seemed to bow inward. They went up a narrow staircase, down a dark hall. The *swish* of traffic moved through the floors, as if the house were an old dog, breathing in its sleep. The boy led the way—running his stick against the wall—and then opened the door with a key he kept under his turtleneck. The apartment itself wasn't much bigger than the boat, and it didn't have the advantage of feeling like a lark—there was a depressing air of permanence to the place. The floor slanted one way, the ceiling sloped the other—there wasn't a right angle to be found in either of the two rooms. The walls looked as soft as taffy—layer upon layer of paint, the current one an odd shade of baby blue. A fluorescent light, of all things, buzzed overhead.

Danny stood on the narrow stretch of carpet between the door and the couch, taking it all in. Suddenly he understood the urgency of treasure. He wished he could say something hopeful, something about how the future would be better if only Carlos studied hard in school, ate his vegetables, and didn't fall into the canal. But everything he tried out sounded hollow—not just disrespectful but also *stupid.*

"Do you want to watch TV?" asked Carlos, pointing with his stick to an enormous console, circa 1970, that took up half the floor space. *His source of information on helicopters,* thought Danny.

"I've got to get back."

"Okay," said the boy. He drew the GI Joe from his belt and climbed up on the couch, which seemed to be upholstered in brown teddy bear fur. "Remember what you said."

"The treasure is yours, pal." Danny moved toward the door. He was suddenly desperate for air—even canal air—but the touch of the doorknob made him stop and turn back. There was more to say, even if he didn't know what it was. "Hey, Carlos, have you ever heard of something called the 'risk-reward ratio'?"

The boy looked at him from his perch on the couch, clearly debating the pros and cons of admitting he hadn't. "No," he said finally.

"It's a very simple concept that expresses—" Danny caught the look of incomprehension and changed direction. "It's a way of balancing what you stand to gain against what you stand to—" Still not right, even with the hand gestures. And then: "It's the dogs versus the treasure."

The boy's face filled with thought, as if he could see the dogs right there, guarding heaps of gold. "The dogs ain't nothing," he said, looking as if he almost believed it.

Yes, a good answer. "You're on salary now," said Danny. "Come by the boat after school tomorrow and I'll give you your first assignment."

—

Back at the boat he remembered his e-mail, and though he didn't feel particularly vengeful at the moment, he booted up anyway. And there it was, a surprisingly lengthy reply posted at 9:28 that morning:

> I hardly know you, Angus, and yet I feel like I've known you a long time already. I probably shouldn't tell you this, but reading your message this morning made me teary, which was bad because I was in a taxi stuck in traffic on the bridge (Palm Pilot! another bad habit, along with cell phones and cigarettes). Tears aren't good for people who wear makeup, and they can get you cashiered from the Society of PR Professionals. It's just that you touched the most important part of me, the part that wants something different, something better. I love children, I love flowers and moose and elk! I envy you.

Children! scoffed Danny, refilling the bowl Carlos had used with more Froot Loops. What did she know about children? Could she explain basic business concepts to an eight-year-old? Did she *employ* any children? Danny Price did! Nevertheless, he found himself feeling magnanimous, even a little sorry for her, and he thought of calling the whole scheme off and letting her go unharmed—until he read what followed:

> Here's another thing I probably shouldn't tell you. I just got out of a bad relationship, and the sense of freedom is still a little overwhelming. I had suppressed my real self for so long, in order to conform to my boyfriend's narrow-minded expectations, I could barely remember who I was anymore. I went through a period of anger, of course, blaming him, and then I realized I'd never recover unless I took responsibility for my own life. Now I only pity him. He sold everything he had and bought a toxic waste dump. I'm sure he fits right in.

Call me whatever you want, thought Danny, *except narrow-minded.* He was now feeling very vengeful indeed. And so he began to type a reply—a long, lyrical reply full of birdsong, sunlight through branches, and the fragrance of mown grass. He got her response at 2:09—it had been written in an elevator in the Chrysler Building—and sent off his answer at 3:52. This last was such a tour de force of gentle wisdom that he printed it out for future reference and taped it to the wall.

What followed over the next few weeks was a series of rapid exchanges, three or four a day, more on weekends, with Clarissa usually writing from work or the back of a taxicab via her Palm Pilot, and Danny typing at his laptop with a somewhat puzzled Carlos looking over his shoulder, offering suggestions.

Danny:

I can't take all the credit, Clarissa, and it's not because I'm so modest, either. Pottery is a collaboration between the potter and the clay. The clay tells me what shape it wants to take, and I supply the hands, that's all. It's really all about listening, the same as with people. The world opens up when you learn to listen.

Clarissa:

When I think about you sitting at the wheel in your potting shed, listening to the clay, I just get a lump in my throat. How beautiful! And then I become ashamed of myself and the life I lead. All I do is talk on the phone—two phones at once, sometimes—and sit in meetings, and get stuck in traffic in the back of taxis. Nobody here listens, least of all me.

Danny:

You listen to me.

Clarissa:

Because you listen to me.

Danny:

Because you have so many beautiful feelings to share.

Clarissa:

I feel I can say anything to you, Angus, and be accepted as who I am. And I want you to know that I accept you as who you are too, no matter what. So let's just get it over with: Why haven't you sent me your picture yet? Is there a reason? I'm not looks-oriented. Do you think I'm that shallow?

Just because you work in PR? For cosmetics firms?

"She probably thinks he's been disfigured," said Danny, turning to Carlos. The boy was seated on the folding table, working his way through yet another bowl of Froot Loops while reading Danny's business plan for the marina.

"These numbers don't add up right," said Carlos, pointing to a row of figures.

"Later with that. Don't you see this is important?"

Danny's solution to the photo problem was to go out and buy a stack of woodworking magazines, as he figured they were the best place to look for anonymous pictures of reasonably fit bearded men in ponytails and work shirts. He and Carlos spent the rest of the evening thumbing their way through issue after issue of *Woodshop* and *Modern Carpenter* until they found the right guy: late thirties, not too handsome, not too ugly, broad shoulders, strong hands—but sensitive.

"Does this look like a truly uninhibited man, unafraid of his own sensual nature?" asked Danny. "Be honest."

"Danny, you're wasting time. We could be rich by now."

"When you're older you'll understand." Danny cut the picture out, snipped off the caption that read *Tom demonstrates proper use of the bandsaw,* scanned it into his computer, and sent it off.

The response came later that night, after he had walked Carlos home:

> The beauty of your soul is right there in your face and in your wonderful, strong hands. You are a good man, Angus. I can see it in your eyes.

Danny sat, peering at the words on the screen—at those two short words in particular: *good man.* He had longed for those words, yearned for them, waited weeks for them, but now that he had them he could only stare with something approaching dismay. What *was* a good man? He didn't know, really, though for the first time in his life he thought that this might be a useful piece of knowledge to possess. Right now, he understood only that it was Clarissa's highest form of praise, and that it meant she was now officially besotted with the fictional Angus Green. His revenge, so carefully cultivated, was ready. All he need do was suggest a meeting.

But that wasn't easy, somehow. He sat, listening to his own breathing, wishing that Carlos were still there. Carlos would have told him what to do. The kid had remarkably good sense for an eight-year-old.

Almost mechanically, he began composing a reply:

> The time has come, Clarissa. I can't wait any longer, I need to see the candlelight reflected in your eyes. Do you know a restaurant in the Village called Madame Lafarge?

This was a little risky; Madame Lafarge had been a favorite of theirs during their courtship, five years earlier. But he felt he could get away with it.

> It's on Charles Street. Meet me there at nine tomorrow night. I'm jumping into the car.

The rats began their nightly scratching at the door. Danny clicked
SEND.

—

Danny twisted on his bunk until the sky lightened, and then finally
fell into a thin, oily sleep, the sort normally associated with fever
and too much cough syrup. The howl of the dogs and the gibber of
the rats infiltrated his dreams. He was driving the dogs away from
Clarissa with a torch. No, he was lighting her on fire. Then he was
pushing her into the canal. She was sinking. He was throwing her a
rope. Rats came running up the rope. He let go. He was at the computer, clicking a button marked SEND.

He didn't see this night of misery as indicative of conflicted feelings, however, only weakness. Ten A.M. found him on his second pot
of coffee, dialing escort services. He was finding out that it isn't
easy to rent a fiancée for a Saturday night in New York, especially
when you have exacting requirements. If this dinner was going to be
the crushing blow he had imagined it to be, he needed to match
Clarissa's vulnerabilities point for point: she was thirty-three, so he
needed twenty-eight; short, so he needed tall; petite, so he needed
buxom; Midwestern, so he needed exotic—preferably with a sexy
accent. Clarissa wore black and never showed skin, so he had to
have a red gown with a slit up the side and significant—meaning
vast, restaurant-disruptive—décolletage. And long red nails. And
stiletto heels. Clarissa would pretend to sneer, but inside she would
crumble.

It was nearly noon when he finally tried an operation called
AAAtractive Escorts. The woman in the photo they e-mailed him
was most certainly attractive, and almost as important, showed evidence of the gown, the heels, and the nails, as well as a lot of up-
swept blond hair. The accompanying spec sheet listed her name as
Olga, her age as twenty-seven (probably shaving three or four years,
thought Danny, but still within parameters), height five-eleven (with
or without hair? he wondered—no way to tell), and bust forty-two.
"And has thick Russian accent," said the very Russian voice over the

phone. "Is what you want, yes?" They were to meet at 8:30 in a coffee shop on Hudson Street and proceed together to the restaurant. "Not to worry, Olga never late." Feeling rather giddy, Danny gave the voice his credit card number.

I get it now, he told himself. *It's just like riding a bicycle. Momentum is your friend.* He called the restaurant and made reservations, one in the name of Angus Green, one in his own, then went back to the Yellow Pages and got the addresses of some rental jewelers, half-surprised that such places really existed. *Christ, you can rent anything in this town,* he muttered, and went to get the car, a bashed-up Toyota he kept locked inside the factory's security fence, camouflaged under tarpaulins and old tires. He dug the car out, got it started, and headed toward the expressway. But something made him stop short at the entrance to the on-ramp—a feeling that momentum alone wouldn't get him over the top and into traffic. He sat for a while, listening to the *swoosh* of cars overhead. Revenge was lonely. He doubled back to Carlos's house.

They took the bridge into Manhattan, Danny driving, the boy sitting in the passenger seat like an oil sheik in his Rolls. He wore those plastic sunglasses, far too large for his face, and an expression of deep satisfaction with the world and its skyscrapers. Danny knew Carlos had been across the river just a handful of times, though he lived only minutes away. To him, this was foreign travel.

"Can we see the stock exchange?" asked Carlos. When Danny went upstairs to get him, the colossal old TV had been tuned to a snowy installment of *Market Watch*.

"Closed on Saturdays," said Danny.

"What about the Empire State Building?"

"Sure, if we have time." Danny drummed his fingers on the steering wheel, distracted by his own turbulent thoughts. "You know, I'm really beginning to feel okay with this," he said. "I'm starting to have fun." But of course this wasn't true. Why couldn't he just relax and enjoy his revenge? he wondered. He had earned it, he deserved to enjoy it. *Not* enjoying it seemed like a kind of character flaw, an inability to appreciate life's gifts. What was wrong with him? Did he want to be a victim all his life? Did he intend to let people step on him forever?

Twenty minutes later they were standing at a counter in a store on Canal Street, looking at rings—jagged knobs of light mounted on circles of gold. "What do you think of this one?" asked Danny, handing it down to Carlos. "It's definitely big." In fact, it looked like a golf ball made of crystal. The saleswoman watched as if this were perfectly ordinary: a man who looked like he'd passed a bad night in the park renting a ring with the help of a boy who kept a GI Joe tucked in his belt. Perhaps it *was* ordinary. The city is big, and human exigencies just about endless. A sign on the wall said RENTAL JEWELRY—THE WORLD'S SECOND OLDEST PROFESSION.

Carlos lifted his sunglasses, then held the ring to the light, squinting. "Looks good to me."

"It's just that she brought this on herself," said Danny. "She dumped me for a cartoon character."

"*You* made him up," said Carlos. They were on the observation deck of the Empire State Building now, the ring in a box in Danny's pocket—radiating some kind of invisible power, lethal as plutonium. He was sweating.

"It was for her own good," he said, holding Carlos up so he could see down. "To show her what a fool she is." The boy was surprisingly small in his arms, and Danny could feel his ribs through the sweatshirt he wore.

"Do you think you could parachute from here?" asked Carlos, trying to press his face through the bars.

"Not without really good insurance." The wind picked up suddenly, and Danny tightened his grip. "The thing is, I'm committed," he said, raising his voice to be heard above the whistle. "Even if I went and confessed the truth, she would never speak to me again. I might as well get it over with and move on. Closure is what I need. Then I can concentrate on the marina."

"What's closure, again?" asked Carlos.

They were back on the boat now, Danny in a suit and tie carefully checked for mold. He was standing by the hot plate but not touching anything—to sit anywhere at all would have resulted in a wet spot. The box with the ring was in his hand, and it seemed to weigh a ton. "Closure is payback," he said. "Closure is inflicting maximal pain."

He checked his watch again. It was 8:15, and he should have left to meet Olga twenty minutes ago. The fact that he couldn't bring himself to step ashore and get in the car made him feel pathetic, and that made him feel angry—at himself. As an antidote, he began mentally cataloguing every injury Clarissa had ever dealt him over the past five years, culminating in the night she walked out of their Brooklyn Heights apartment—the ultimate act of betrayal. But none of it got him closer to opening the door. He began pacing up and down the tiny cabin—two steps forward, two steps back. "What's a good man, Carlos?"

"How should I know? I'm just a kid."

"Don't give me that crap."

The boy spoke as if reciting a lesson from memory. "A good investor balances risk and reward."

"You get that from one of your programs?"

"I got it from you."

"And what the hell does it mean?" This last was a shout of frustration directed at the ceiling.

"It means it's okay to be scared of the dogs."

Danny stopped. The boy was sitting on the bunk in his jeans and a sweatshirt, the glasses perched on his head, a half-drunk bottle of Coke propped in his lap. He had no parents, as far as Danny could tell, and a sister who worked two jobs and was hardly ever home. His playground was a toxic canal infested with rats, and his sustaining dream the discovery of buried treasure where there was none. He knew the dogs.

Danny glanced at his watch. It was 8:39. He pictured Clarissa in the back of a taxi on her way to the restaurant, peering nervously into a little pocket mirror, checking her teeth for lipstick. Was she so wrong to feel the time slipping away? How much time do we have to make things right with each other, anyway? He pictured the never-late Olga, decked out in her red gown, finishing a cup of truly execrable coffee in that diner on Hudson Street. Perhaps she was thinking about calling in to her dispatcher; perhaps she was simply lost in nostalgic memories of winter in Vladivostok. Forget her; she had been paid in advance, she would go on to her next out-call. And forget Angus Green. He would go on growing virtual Swiss chard in his virtual garden forever. He was of no relevance to the here and now, to life on the canal.

"Have you ever had French food, Carlos?"

"Will I like it?"

"You seem to like everything else. Besides, there's somebody I want you to meet." He took the boy's hand, and together they started for the door.

CALISTA X

Alexander Parsons

"She send you any naked pictures?" Xavier asked.

"Don't talk about her like that," Jake said. "It's disrespectful."

"Disrespectful."

It sounded as stilted to Jake as it did to Xavier, but he meant it. Calista was a private matter. He picked at the label on his bottle of Bohemia.

"*Oígame, pendejo,*" Xavier said. "Disrespectful is when I drive three hours to get your ass to your date and you won't tell me shit about her." Xavier had deep-set eyes and pale skin that stretched tautly over his severe features. Ten years older than Jake, he treated him with the aggressive condescension of a loyal and cruel elder brother.

Put that way it did seem rude, though Jake knew anything he told Xavier would just be used for ammunition in some later conversation.

"Where the fuck is the entertainment?" Xavier said. They'd been sitting in Prince Machiavelli's for an hour, killing time before Jake's date with Calista. Jake was afraid Xavier would make him late getting to the hotel where they were to meet. When Xavier drank he got very enthusiastic over women, and so a strip club was likely to be the last place he'd want to leave, especially early on a Friday night. Jake didn't want to be here, not alone and especially not with Xavier in the hours before he was to see Calista for the first time. But his Impala had needed a new clutch and the use of Xavier's truck came with conditions, the primary one being Xavier's company. They worked together for the highway department in a small New Mexican town three hours north of El Paso; Xavier had been as eager as Jake to escape for the weekend.

"Maybe there's a stripper's union: no thongs until after five. Those things can't be comfortable," Jake said. He wanted to get to the hotel and change out of his work clothes, which were covered with the asphalt they'd tamped into potholes that morning. "Or maybe they're on strike," he added, hopeful.

"I ain't going to keep paying five bucks a beer if we don't get to see no titties."

Jake didn't point out that it was *his* debit card paying the bill. He rearranged the bottles on the table like a glass picket fence. He was already anxious even though Calista wouldn't be free from work until after seven. She was a buyer for U-Wear, a company in Manhattan that made clothes—mainly T-shirts and underwear. ("Fruit-of-the-Loom-type stuff," she'd written. "Don't get your hopes up.") They were looking to establish contacts with one of the *maquiladoras* in Juárez and had sent her to El Paso for the week. She and Jake had met two months earlier via an eBay exchange when he'd bought some comics she'd inherited from a cousin. This was to be their first face-to-face encounter.

"So you don't even know what she looks like," Xavier said.

"She sent me a picture."

"Let's see."

"I don't have it here," Jake lied. He carried a portrait of Calista in his wallet, but the computer printout gave her face an orange tint and the resolution wasn't sharp. Add to these the quality of the paper, and it was more a photo of the idea of her than any real likeness.

Still, he loved to study it, imagining the variations of emotion and expression that might play over her features in his company, at his comments.

"I bet you got it taped above your bed," Xavier said. "And I bet she's naked and has big tits." Xavier had been prying for details all afternoon and such unrelenting and vaguely proprietary interest had made Jake paranoid. He was protective of Calista in a way he couldn't explain to Xavier, not so he'd understand.

"It's not that kind of picture."

"But she's hot," Xavier said.

"Fuck," said Jake. "I don't know. Yeah. Sure. I guess."

"Don't pretend with me, *ése*. This is all about sex. You don't talk to some girl for two months just so you can meet and have a *conversation*."

Jake wanted to deny it, but there was truth to this. Since he and Calista had started e-mailing there had been a lot of flirting, and he had been undeniably relieved when her photo showed her to be attractive, if a little gaunt. On the nights he corresponded with her a sexual charge crackled through the ritual. He would call up the exchanges of the past weeks and then begin to read, pausing to repeat certain phrases, compliments, and observations aloud, pondering the implications of endings that read "yours" or "love," his lips moving slightly as he murmured this liturgy, his face rapt as he wrote to the woman he imagined. Had they been sending actual letters, he would have smelled the pages for hints of her perfume, touched his tongue to the envelope flaps, perhaps carried them in the breast pocket of his shirt.

This, then, was the remove from which Jake experienced his romance. When he'd first encountered the Internet, many of his evenings had consisted of rote masturbation before the wanton gazes of various naked women: white, Hispanic, black, Asian, thick-limbed and thin, a wide variety that quickly took on a shallow uniformity as they played across his screen.

Which was not to say that this time was without its value. While initially convinced that his interest was a singularly unhealthy obsession, that he was fast becoming a watery-eyed pervert bound to haunt playgrounds and public restrooms or get caught fucking the neighbor's Doberman, his interest began to flag. He began to view the experience as a more-or-less-harmless voyage into the seas of his sexuality that had, at this point, left him stranded on the shores of normalcy. In the wake of many fears, he'd come to the conclusion that he was depressingly average and predictable in his tastes: no latex, fat, amputee, or foot fetishes; no interest in the elderly, the juvenile, or the pregnant; no interest in the neighbor's dog. It was true that his eyes skipped from photos of naked men with a rapidity that belied comfort, but there didn't seem much more to it, or at least nothing that wasn't easily repressed. He had discovered an indifference to breast size (he more or less liked them all); to hair color, to panty and bra style. In sum, these many hours spent in the taboo waters of the cyber world had left him with the less-than-profound realization that he was a legs-and-ass man. What was less clear, but beginning to emerge from the murk in the course of his explorations, was that he needed more than this superficial sexual reckoning with the female. Calista, in the form of her enduring electronic presence and interest, had stimulated in him an overwhelming appetite for substantive romance.

Three of the strippers entered through the smoked-glass double doors. That, Jake thought, or they were attractive women who'd gotten very lost. All of the men turned to look at them. Xavier stood and clapped his hands. "Hey, what are you doing dressed?" he said.

Two looked annoyed, but one flashed their table.

"You make me a happy man!" Xavier shouted over the smattering of applause from the other men.

"We should get to the hotel," Jake said.

"*Fuck* no," Xavier said. "Those women will be naked soon."

"So what?" Jake said. "It's not like you're going to get a date out of it. They won't even kiss you."

"You better hope you're wrong," Xavier said. "Otherwise I might end up in bed with your woman."

Jake walked out to the parking lot to get his duffel, which held his clothes for the weekend, irritated that Xavier could annoy him so effortlessly. The lot of Prince Machiavelli's overlooked eight lanes of rushing traffic on I-10 and, farther afield, the endless sprawl of Juárez. The club was a stucco structure with towers and crenellations like oversize Lego blocks. Jake hoisted his duffel, resigned to changing in the club's bathroom.

In the men's room he practiced saying Calista's name, settling on a tone that, he imagined, implied he was meeting an old friend and confidant, an ex-lover with whom the romance was ready to spark again. In the face of such expectations, any doubts over the fact that they had, in fact, never met were easily ignored. He wondered what she'd think of him. The light dusting of acne and his startled eyes accented his youth without detracting from his looks. He wet a hand and pressed it to his tousled blond hair. He hadn't aged much in the ten years since finishing high school.

When he returned he found that Xavier had ordered them another round. The bass thump of techno racketed against the walls and made him wish he'd brought aspirin. He looked around, unhappy to be grouped with the losers sitting near them. Windowless and dimly lit, Prince Machiavelli's smelled of air freshener, smoke, sweat, and male desperation. Most of the men were stationed around the stage, where a chunky stripper now performed a desultory bump-and-grind against a chrome pole.

Near them a man sat enduring a lap dance. There was no other way to phrase it. A woman in a thong gyrated her ass inches from his nose. He sat motionless, his hands on his thighs, his face like a wood mask, as if his impassivity would somehow distance him from the vulgar, public spectacle his libido demanded. The dancer's face was equally impassive, though with a genuine lack of interest. She popped her gum, chewing to the repetitive beat of the music, perhaps organizing a to-do list in her head.

Jake began to laugh, realizing how nervous he was. He pointed at the pair when Xavier looked at him.

"An ass in your face ain't nothing to laugh at," Xavier said with mock solemnity.

Jake admitted that there were moments when Xavier was all

right. He toasted his companion, feeling for a moment generous and superior. The prospect of the evening insulated him from the lonely apathy of the club. It was possible to believe he had nothing in common with these other men. Xavier seemed to sense this and immediately went on the offensive.

"Maybe she's a man," he said. "Some fucked-up dude, you know? Just pretending." He grinned at this, liking the story. "And then, *ése*, you know, you think something's not right, but it's not until you're reaching down there," he grabbed his crotch, "when you realize she's, you know, all man. And better hung than you!" he added with a flourish.

"Is this your date?" Jake asked. "Is she your girlfriend? Are you having drinks with her tonight?"

"I'm just saying," Xavier said, draining his beer and reaching for Jake's.

"I already know her," Jake said. "She isn't some chick with a dick." He wondered how late he'd be for the date he'd been anticipating for more than a month.

———

Two hours later Jake exited the bathroom of the Camino Real Hotel with his attention fixed on his crotch. He'd leaked a little while zipping up and had tried to dry his pants against the hand dryer, but this had been painfully hot and he'd been afraid someone would catch him at it. As he walked down the hall wishing the sconce lights were dimmer, he saw Calista: he uttered her name without thinking.

She was on her cell phone and didn't seem to hear him. He repeated her name, but it was the fact that he stood in her path to the bathroom that got her attention.

She held up her hand and turned away for a moment, trying to refocus on the call. She hunched a shoulder, shielding the phone from him.

Nonplussed, Jake let his hand fall to his side and stood witnessing the first of the evening's collisions between the hoped-for and the actual. There was an unsettling mix of the familiar and strange about her. He recognized her face, minus the orange tint of his photo, but her kohled eyes and the complex knot of her dark hair, which looked to have two chopsticks stuck in it, were exotic, part of a style wholly unfamiliar to him. When she turned to face him, he saw in her neck that she was older than he had supposed, older and tired, with pallid skin that accented the smudged sleeplessness beneath her eyes.

She smiled at him. "Sorry," she said, "but no one's called me that out loud."

"Calista?" he asked.

"It's my nom de plume," she said. He didn't know what this meant and didn't ask. She shook his hand in an oddly formal manner that made him feel as if they were both at work.

Xavier caught sight of Jake from the main room and headed for him. He moved with the slow deliberation of the very drunk. "Hey," he said, "you see if they got condom machines in the bathrooms?"

Jake was mortified. He shrugged. Xavier seemed not to notice Calista as he moved toward the bathrooms. "I shouldn't loan so many out," he said over his shoulder.

"Do you know that guy?" Calista asked.

Jake shook his head. "I mean, we work together, but that's it. I don't know what he's doing here."

Calista nodded, unconvinced. "I'm sitting at the bar. Why don't you wait for me there?" And with that she brushed past him and into the bathroom.

Jake sat at the bar, eager to leave with Calista before Xavier showed up again. Xavier liked to goad him and would be impossible to get rid of once he realized who Calista was. Goading was a basic component of their difficult friendship. Jake absently patted at his pocket, feeling the two condoms Xavier had flipped to him when they'd arrived at their room.

The bar of the Camino Real was square with high stools, set directly beneath a vaulted ceiling, the apex a dome of Tiffany stained glass that bathed the room with blue light and made the patrons look as if they were underwater. The walls were faced with polished marble, the floor carpeted. The space felt like old Mexico with an undertone of Motel 6. Jake sat near a heavyset man who gripped his wide-mouth Bud Light fiercely, as if it were a cleat attached to an unsteady boat deck. On the TV screen fixed atop the low shelves of liquor and glasses, a parched Clint Eastwood stumbled over a series of dunes and through the script of a bad spaghetti western, the sun tilting crazily above.

He turned to watch for Calista, seeing her as she entered the main room. Her stride was quick and efficient, not at all similar to the sensuously languorous sway he'd imagined. He was trying to decide whether he found her attractive when he noticed that the guy beside him had spun around.

"Did you two meet?" Calista asked. "Bernie, Jake. Jake, Bernie."

"Bernie," Jake said. It came out like a question. Bernie's suit was tight in the shoulders and thighs. He was swollen with middle age and too much beer. He had on spectacularly ugly cowboy boots that looked to be made from a bumpy reptile the orange of Gatorade.

Bernie inclined his head the barest amount. "You want another Manhattan, Miss New York?"

"She likes gin martinis," Jake said, "without the olive and with Tanqueray Malacca gin." He thought she'd be impressed that he'd remembered this detail, but she looked taken aback, as if he'd said something indelicate.

"Manhattan?" Bernie asked again.

"That's a nice ring," Jake said, pointing to the nondescript wedding band on Bernie's ring finger.

"Keep pushing," Bernie said, taking a moment to stare hard at Jake.

"I'll take a rain check this time," Calista said to Bernie, her voice soft. She gave him a small smile.

"You sure?" Bernie looked askance at Jake.

Calista nodded.

This time, Jake repeated to himself. He wasn't particularly attracted to Calista but he felt keenly jealous. As he touched her shoulder to guide her toward the street exit a look of annoyance briefly creased her face and he dropped his hand. She'd said in an early e-mail that she liked it when a guy would take charge on a date: "Forget all that sensitive 90s crap," she'd written. "I want someone to take care of me when I go out. I want to relax." But here it was and he couldn't even take her arm. The night had been derailed and he had no idea where they were heading.

"How do you know that guy?" he asked, keeping an eye out for Xavier as they exited.

"He's no different from the friend you brought from work," said Calista. "A little protection."

"I was just using him for his car," Jake said.

"Don't worry about it," Calista said. "I might have been someone you wanted to avoid."

The Stanton Street Bridge into Juárez, only a few blocks from the hotel, was thick with traffic. Scraps of Spanish floated by as people passed them on the sidewalk. Jake was more aware of his surroundings. Shredded plastic bags fluttered in the light wind, caught in the concertina wire strung atop the walls and fences abutting the road. Idling cars waited to pass through customs, their exhaust washing through the air. He paid a quarter for each of them at the tollbooth and they headed up the bridge's incline.

"Scenic," said Calista. She adjusted her purse, one hand firmly gripping the strap, the other buttoning her light jacket. In dress, at least, she was what Jake had expected: lots of black. She wore leather pants, a billowy blouse of some darkly iridescent material, and wobbly shoes that looked hard on the ankles. High-rent and urban, she probably hadn't planned on walking into Juárez for the night.

Beneath the bridge the dark, sluggish trickle of the Rio Grande gleamed in its concrete channel. "So that's the mighty river," Calista said, pausing to look down at it. "The Rio Grande," she said with an exaggerated drawl.

"Scenic, right?" Jake said, a little hurt that she seemed set on resisting the night. He'd been mulling over her silence and her comment. *Scenic.* The sarcasm of the statement, of the lack it implied, seemed to be an indictment of him as well. Even her faux drawl seemed aimed at him. "Sarcasm is the refuge of the cynic," he said.

"Is that so?"

"You wrote that," he said.

"Did I?" Calista looked alarmed by this news. It didn't occur to Jake that the alarm might have some other source. She touched her jacket pocket where Jake had seen her put her phone. "Do you remember everything I write?" she asked.

Jake shook his head. "Only what I reread twenty times." He meant it as a compliment, a joke, a way of breaking the tension between them. But she looked further taken aback, not flattered. She was more inaccessible than her e-mails had made her seem, more abrupt, harder edged. He saw that he'd had definite, if unuttered, expectations for the evening and for her, expectations that did not include the actual woman walking beside him. Maybe if he'd lingered in the bar of the Camino Real, Xavier could have taken his place.

"So everything I send you is on the record?"

"I guess," Jake said, not liking the way she made it sound. They resumed walking. A woman in a shawl pleaded with them in a high, plaintive voice, her hand outstretched.

"Is it okay to use American money?" Calista asked.

Jake smiled, glad for this soft spot in the carapace of her sophistication. He took some change from his pocket and placed it in the woman's palm. "Juárez runs on dollars," he said.

A mufflerless truck rattled past, an immense pile of flattened cardboard boxes swaying on its bed. "I like what you write," Jake said. "That's why I reread."

Calista looked at him curiously, her face unreadable. She wasn't afraid of eye contact. "I like yours, too," she said. "They're guileless. Like you sit down and write exactly what comes to mind."

In fact, Jake slaved over his missives, a dictionary and thesaurus at hand. He would reread a string of Calista's, warming up to their exchanges and attempting to don the same air of cosmopolitan offhandedness he so loved in her writing. "My parents always said I was simple," he said. Her smile slightly eased his disappointment.

Calista's phone rang, the tune of beeps the theme song to the Lone Ranger. Jake tried not to interpret it as another slight.

"Work," she said, and then stepped away from him to talk. Jake leaned against the bridge railing with his thumbs hooked in his pockets. She wasn't attractive exactly, at least not in the way he was used to measuring such things. But with her that seemed only a portion of an equation he didn't understand how to work. It was a blind date with insanely high expectations, he admitted. And without the refuge of small talk to explore: music, food, and astrological signs had already been well trod in the course of their electronic exchanges.

Once she'd ended her call they passed through the turnstiles and onto Juárez Avenue. A few cabdrivers called out to them in English. "You'll like Martino's," Jake said. "It's really good French food."

"French cuisine in Juárez," Calista said. She touched her jacket pocket.

"Watch your step," Jake said, as he shepherded her past a deep, unmarked pit that had been dug in the sidewalk. A water main showed a few feet down. "More scenery," he added.

Martino's, though, was a big hit with Calista. From the moment one of the old waiters, courtly and grave in his black jacket, mixed a martini for her tableside, she began to enjoy herself. And Calista was a wonderful drunk. She drank with the enthusiasm of someone playing a sport she enjoyed. The alcohol seemed to smooth the harder and more unforgiving angles of her personality. She smiled more, and her sarcasm was less disdainful than mischievous.

"Do you really clean up roadkill?" she asked as their food arrived.

Jake grinned at the reference. It was a joke she often alluded to in her e-mails. "It's good eating," he said indignantly. "Better even than this." He pointed his fork at his steak. In truth, picking up roadkill was an occasional duty at the New Mexico Department of Transportation. Recently killed deer and the like was put in cold storage for the wolves at the Alamogordo Zoo. "Mainly, though," he continued, "we whistle at chicks." He'd joined her in drinking martinis, and though he didn't like their taste, three had suffused him with a warmth and confidence he longed to share. He motioned for the waiter and ordered a bottle of Pouilly-Fuissé, badly mangling the French.

"Let's hear your whistle," Calista said. Jake laughed, hearing in this the flirtatious confidence he so liked in her e-mails.

"Okay," Jake said, "but you'll have to lean in close. It's not very loud."

Calista slid closer to Jake in the crescent-shaped booth, brushing a stray lock of her hair behind her ear, the universal gesture of a woman who knows she's being admired.

A street photographer with a Polaroid camera approached their table. *"Quieren un photo?"* he asked, his voice sadly hopeful.

Calista put her arm around Jake's neck. "Evidence," she said. The camera flashed. As they waited for the image to sharpen, Calista's phone rang again. Jake paid for the photo, annoyed. Calista talked while he drank a glass of wine. She apologized when she finished, fiddling with the buttons before replacing it in her jacket. "It won't ring now," she explained. She lifted her glass and sipped at the wine. "So," she said, attempting to pick up the rhythm of the conversation, "if I walked by where you were working would you whistle at me?"

"I would," Jake said, pretty sure he'd lied. It was true, though, that talking with her like this and hearing in their conversation the resonance of their past e-mail made it easier to overlook the fact that she didn't match the contours of his imagined date.

"Maybe I'd whistle back," she said. The noise of the restaurant flowed into the pocket of silence at their table as they considered the lies that had brought them together for this night of pleasurable disappointment.

For Jake, the exchange marked the complex tone of the evening, a moment somehow better even than the return trip to the bridge when he held Calista's hand, the delicate bird weight of it making him feel fiercely protective as they unsteadily headed to the pedestrian border check.

The intimacy of handholding, though, was interrupted as they passed through the heavy, translucent plastic curtains that marked the entrance to the air-conditioned chill of U.S. Customs. There, the two of them were questioned and asked to empty their pockets. One of the guards sorted through Calista's purse. They were polite about it, but that didn't do much to offset the awkwardness. Jake had to place his wallet and the twin squares of foil-wrapped Trojans, extra thin for sensitivity, on the Bakelite table beside Calista's phone and mace canister. Her phone was set to vibrate and a call came in, which made it skitter about like an angry sex toy. Jake wondered if the mace was for protection from him, realizing that this was what she'd been touching for reassurance when her hand had brushed her jacket pocket over the course of the evening.

What really caught his attention, though, was the photo of a young boy in her datebook, just opposite her sheathed credit cards. His face bore a striking resemblance to hers. She'd never mentioned children or nephews. Did she have a husband? An ex? Her ring finger was bare, but what did that prove? It seemed like he ought to know who the kid was, and as he thought on this he wondered what else remained unseen behind the illusory image of Calista's life that e-mail had provided him. The sight of the condoms beside the mysterious photo then set him thinking in another way: Did a kid mean stretch marks? C-section scars? He didn't even know what those would look like. And had she not told him for fear that a child would scare him away? What did that imply about what she wanted? Was there a whole part of her life he knew nothing about? It felt like a betrayal, though he knew it shouldn't, and at that moment their epistolary history felt like nothing so much as strands to a web that both bound them together and impeded their freedom of motion.

———

At the Camino Real, Xavier sat watching a local football game. Jake was relieved to see him; he felt he needed a break from Calista, especially after the awkwardness of the border check. They'd hardly said a word for the remainder of the walk.

"No wonder he runs home to check his mail every night," Xavier said by way of introduction. He placed his hands on Calista's shoulders, as if to hold her steady so that he might memorize her face. His dark eyes glittered with sexual appetite. "He won't even go out for drinks after work until after he's checked to see if you wrote." They all settled at a low table ringed with armchairs.

"You'll have to excuse me a moment," Calista said, bringing out her phone, which was vibrating again. She walked away from them, searching for better reception.

"She ain't bad," Xavier said.

"Pretty hot," Jake said, though he didn't know if he believed it. There was an insistent, nagging feeling that he was impelled to act this way simply because of their history, and not out of genuine attraction. He wondered who'd called her. It seemed too late for work.

"*Hot,*" Xavier said. "At least say it like you mean it."

"Maybe I'm just sobering up," Jake said.

Xavier fixed him with a look of unalloyed contempt. "That's your damn problem, *pendejo.* You always got to find something wrong. Me? Like, take Teresa: sure, she's got a fat ass, but that pussy feels *good.*" Teresa was Xavier's sometime girlfriend.

"I don't even know what that's supposed to mean," Jake said. He'd thought about Teresa's pussy, though.

"You need tequila," Xavier counseled.

"She's, like, forty," Jake said.

"What are you, some fucking belladonna?"

"Prima donna," Jake said.

"She ain't forty," Xavier said. He opened her purse and pulled out her organizer to find her license.

"Put that away," Jake hissed, looking over his shoulder for Calista. She had her back to them, the phone to her ear.

"*Tranquilo,*" Xavier said, flipping through it. Then he slipped it back. "She ain't no older than you," he announced.

Jake didn't believe him but wasn't about to look for himself. "Whatever," he said. He felt tired, too tired to try to explain to either himself or Xavier why it was that he wanted to leave.

Xavier leaned in and slapped him, hard enough that it stung even through the numbness of the booze.

"What the fuck?" Jake said, rubbing his cheek. A few people had looked over at the sound.

"Pay attention," Xavier said. He'd done the same thing to Jake a few times at work. Jake got spacey, as if what was going on around him didn't matter. Such distraction incensed Xavier, who often said that Jake's problem was that he never seemed to have a stake in his own life. Or, in Xavier's words: "You fuck around too much. You have to know what you want and take it."

He rubbed at his cheek, debating the merits of hitting back. He knew Xavier hadn't slapped him out of malice. The first time this had happened he'd punched Xavier and had understood then, as he did now, that their friendship was compelling partly because neither could explain it. The undercurrent of rivalry flecked with abuse should have made it untenable, but instead made it singular.

A year past, Jake and Xavier had driven down to El Paso because the Miss America pageant was in town and Xavier wanted to "fuck Miss Wisconsin." The contestants had been staying at this very hotel, and Xavier had strode in, absurd in his feed cap and too-tight Wrangler jeans in the middle of so much milling formal wear, looking like an underdressed matador. Jake had been keenly aware of the way those women looked at his friend as he tried to chat them up. He had lingered back at the bar, marveling at Xavier's imperviousness to their brittle smiles and the fact that they would turn away even when he was in midsentence. It wasn't so much that Xavier didn't notice such slights, but that he didn't care, not as long as he got what he was after—which was, in this case, to get laid. In the end, Xavier's stalwart persistence had paid off: he had spent the night with one of the staff, a beautifully curvaceous woman whose weight gave her face a sexy pout. Jake, in an adjacent room, had had to listen in disbelief to the muted thump of their lovemaking through most of the night.

"She isn't Miss Wisconsin," Jake warned before walking to the bathroom. He needed a moment to collect himself. He avoided eye contact with Calista on his way around the bar, in part because he was feeling guilty, suspecting that they had been searched because he was wearing undershot Mexican heels on his cowboy boots, a style generally considered suspicious on an Anglo. He wondered if she'd seen Xavier strike him.

Preoccupied, he'd lined up at the urinal before noticing the other man in the bathroom. He was talking on his cell phone and at first Jake thought he was zipping up at the sinks, hearing as he did the clink of belt buckle. As he committed to his pissing, though, he realized that the little guy was jacking off.

"What about for lunch," the guy said. "Where'd you go?" The conversation continued along this line, the man laconic, distracted, and insistent. Jake didn't understand how the description of what was clearly someone's day was worthy of masturbation, much less in a public bathroom. As he walked out he had the urge to tell the guy to use a stall. In the mirror he saw the man's face: a pockmarked face with sad parentheses etched on either side of a thin mouth that was, for the moment, fixed in a beatific smile. His eyes were closed. "And then?" he asked. Unsure of why, Jake made an effort to leave silently.

——

"Don't take it that way," Xavier said. "He gets like that with everyone. It don't mean nothing." Jake had circled the bar to approach Xavier and Calista from behind, vaguely paranoid and wanting to hear what Xavier was saying. He felt bad for this when he realized that Xavier was trying to get him laid, talking him up to this woman he didn't think he wanted to be with. And that Xavier was doing so said something else: that Jake wasn't necessarily what she'd hoped for, either. He lingered behind the high-backed armchairs, feeling grateful and depressed.

The bar was closing as they finished their drinks. Xavier looked around at the departing couples, sighting a single woman still planted on her bar stool. "It's the hour for action," Xavier said, rising. He reached out to shake Calista's hand, pulling her up and hugging her instead. He winked at Jake over her shoulder. Jake gave him the finger. After he had departed Jake and Calista regarded each other. Jake crunched a piece of ice. "So," he said. But she leaned forward and touched a finger to his lips, stilling his words. She tapped her fingernail once against his teeth and he felt his breath catch. Then she took his hand.

Jake glanced back, to where Xavier leaned against the bar. Their eyes met and Xavier grabbed his crotch and made a pumping motion with his arm.

In her room they kissed and gradually removed each other's clothes. She wore silken red panties and no bra. "Those don't look like company issue," Jake said. Her skin was very smooth and felt impossibly warm.

Calista's phone began to vibrate on the bedside table. She reached for it and pressed a button. The luminescent face went black.

"I thought it might have been something else," Jake joked, trying to hide his annoyance. He took the phone from her and rose from the bed. His erection tented the fabric of his boxers. He left the phone on the bathroom counter and closed the door. "Who keeps calling?" he asked.

"Let's keep those condoms from wearing a hole in your pocket," Calista said. She kissed his ear, tracing it with her tongue. He shivered and closed his eyes. He realized he didn't know her name and smiled in the dark: Xavier could tell him in the morning.

"You smell like smoke," Calista said. "I thought you didn't smoke."

"I don't," Jake said, thinking back to Prince Machiavelli's. He wished he'd had time to shower.

"Do you really keep a photo of me above your bed?"

Jake laughed. "Xavier said that?"

"He said a lot of things."

She reached down to grasp him. They moved together in the indeterminate dark, naked and free, for the moment, of the concerns and doubts that would reassert themselves with first light. Sex was as awkward and pleasurable as the first time with someone new invariably is, and this was good, reassuring for both of them. In this, at least, there was not the pretense of familiarity that had marred much of the evening.

After sex Calista handed him the photo from Martino's. "Xavier said the one you keep in your wallet makes me look orange."

Jake shook his head. He could tell by her voice that she was flattered. He wondered when, in the past months, Xavier had gone through his wallet and found it, and what combination of truth and lies Xavier had told her. Jake stroked her hair, now free of the chopsticks. It was thick and luxurious. Gradually they relaxed into sleep.

Come morning, the desert light slanted through the parted curtains, harshly beautiful, candescent white where it touched the bedsheets. Calista lay breathing silently. Jake stood watching her. Her face showed the abrasion of age in its fine wrinkles. He leaned in to kiss her chastely on the forehead, not wanting to wake her. As he did she opened her eyes. They were the soft gray of flannel and filled with what he thought was a heartbreaking vulnerability and equanimity. They regarded each other and the silence magnified. Jake leaned in again to kiss her on the lips, filled with an unexpected and genuine love, and as he did Calista offered her cheek and a wan smile.

—

Xavier swerved toward a rattlesnake on the road's shoulder, just missing it. The truck's hood was a blinding panel of reflected light beyond which the desert air warped under the weight of the midday heat. They were an hour into the drive back to Cornucopia, each hungover and thoughtful.

Jake handed Xavier the photo. "That's us in Juárez," he said.

"She was hot," Xavier said. "Especially for forty-one."

Jake paused. "Thanks for that update. You think maybe you can tell me her name, too? I mean, now that she's gone and it won't do me any good?"

"Nah," Xavier said with a grin. He made to hand the photo back.

Jake shook his head, smiling in spite of himself. "It's yours," he said to his friend.

ENDPOINT

Po Bronson

I've known her for three days. The plane to Montreal leaves in six hours. What do I do?

In three days it is already so close to love. By tomorrow it would be love. If I don't say the words, I will burst. But tomorrow I will be in Montreal, beginning the rest of my life.

"Jennifer Jennifer Jenny," I say, each word with a slightly different intonation, the string a cryptic sentence of philosophy.

"What?" She smiles. I've teased her.

"Six hours."

"I know," she whispers empathically, feeling as hopeless as I.

If it was love, really love, we would know what to do.

Coming this close in just three days is damn good. Makes a man wonder.

Six hours.

"Make time stand still again," she begs, and I can tell that when I do, she will start to cry.

—

You wake up in the middle of the night and it feels like your mouth is sewn closed. You panic. You cannot open your mouth to scream for help. It feels like if you force your jaws open, you will tear the roof of your mouth off. The involuntary reaction of the muscles in the neck and cheeks is to squeeze the salivary glands and swallow, but the glands are dead and it feels like you just swallowed a two-by-four. The application of topical artificial saliva takes thirty minutes just to get the mouth open in the morning. Talking is brutally painful. Telling those who've come to see you die that you love them is impossible.

I've been there in the room. A hundred times.

"He wants to tell you he loves you," I want to say.

It's like watching the worst stutter imaginable. *Come on, you can say it.*

His eyes plead, *I want to say it one more time.*

I know, I know.

"Don't talk, Daddy," they say. "It's okay."

He needs to say it, has to say it.

"He wants to tell you he loves you," I want to say.

"His mouth is just too dry right now," I say. "Come back in an hour."

His eyes look to me. He's begging me. Those eyes are screaming. Fix it so I can say it one last time.

None of this is in the data.

You wake up in the middle of the night with your mouth sewn closed.

The condition is called Xerostomia.

I cannot save them, but I can grant them a dying wish.

This is what I must get across.

Four out of five will die anyway.

That's the catch.

I have looked into too many eyes.

—

I come to Washington, D.C., to present my data. Four times a year, the Food and Drug Administration convenes a panel of twelve eminent oncologists to advise the FDA on which new cancer drugs to approve for sale. Ninety-nine times out of a hundred, the FDA accepts the panel's recommendation. If Ethyol is approved, first year sales are anticipated to be over $200 million, and I will move to Montreal to continue research into other uses of Ethyol. There are significant tax advantages to doing research in Canada. I already have the plane ticket. I already have the lab space leased. I already have an old girlfriend there waiting for me. She's expecting me to move in. It won't be a conscious choice; I'll simply stay with her "until I get my own place," which I never will. We're going to try again and, this time, get it right.

The panel convenes for three days in the grand ballroom of the Town Center Hotel in Silver Springs, Maryland. Swank it is not. Think traveling salesmen anonymity. Think threadbare carpets, hollow walls, maids vacuuming at odd hours, art bolted to the walls so it can't be stolen. I show up two days before my time slot, book a conference room down the hall from the panel hearings, and begin rehearsing with my staff and various $2,500-a-day consultants. The double doors are open to the hall.

"It's no use," I say, dropping flat, holding my weary head in my hands.

Why not? everyone demands to know.

"Only the data matters." Nothing I can say will make a difference.

"Of course it will."

"Four out of five die anyway."

"But you help them."

"There's nothing about helping them in the data." Quality of life cannot be measured.

One notion, seven years of development, one hour in front of the panel.

Sixty million dollars and four clinical trials.

This has been a huge waste.

I'm going to fail.

Then Jennifer walks by. I fall backward into a huge down pillow.

"Who was that?" Linda says.

I don't have any idea.

"She looked at you like she knew you."

I would have remembered meeting a woman like her. That's not a connection a man can forget.

I am going with my instinct here.

"Excuse me, guys. Can we break for fifteen?"

I pace down the hall, dart into the ballroom where the committee was hearing an Upjohn presentation. She is sitting in the back row. Alone. We whisper.

"Hi."

"Hi."

I am rolling in that big down pillow in the morning light.

"Wow."

"What?"

"We haven't met before?"

"No."

Little things add up fast: skin, smile, size, warmth, softness, confidence, keenness in the eyes. Body language, mostly. She doesn't feel like a stranger. Already I want to have babies with her.

"Will you touch my hand?" I put my palm out, resting on my thigh.

"Why?"

"I don't know. I just feel compelled that we should touch."

"Okay."

I am going on instinct here.

She puts her hand down flat on mine.

"Take it away if you feel at all uncomfortable," I offer.

"No, it's okay."

The current runs between us.

That's not a connection a man can forget.

A man waits his whole life for that kind of clarity.

———

I've known her for three days. The plane to Montreal leaves in five hours.

Okay, I get on the plane. When I get off the plane, Jo is waiting for me with flowers. Waiting for me I can take, but the flowers are too much. She can tell by my reaction that I'm uncomfortable with the flowers. I've been in Canada two minutes and already off to a bad start. Flowers mean nothing to me but dressing up death. I take the flowers and get on the long people mover and feel like I'm being carted to my death, all dressed up.

At her apartment, there's hot water for tea on simmer. The corners of the bedding are turned back. The oval mirror where we can watch ourselves make love is aimed at the bed. A deep bowl of bow-tie pasta salad chills in the refrigerator. There's beer, too. And in the bathroom, a second toothbrush. Jo was so ready for me. So ready for me that now she's embarrassed, and in the car on the way to her apartment she's afraid her apartment will be like the flowers, too much too soon.

"You want to just drive around for a while?" she says.

She drives up to Regent's Park. The students have just been let out of school and are running wild. They barely wear anything. We walk around. Jo is so nice to me. I feel so guilty. I feel ruined. I'll spend years trying to forget a woman I knew only for three days.

—

I've known her for three days. The plane to Montreal leaves in five hours.

I go to the airport. I get my boarding pass. But I never get on the plane. I tell my investors I'm sorry. Seven years has been enough. Time for something new. I tell them I'm going to North Carolina.

"What will you do there?"

I don't know. Find something. An old door closes, a new door opens. Start fresh.

"But why?"

I refuse to explain it to them.

"You're too impulsive," they tell me. "You always were."

I call Jo. I tell her I'm not coming to Montreal. I'm afraid she'll cry, but instead she's furious. If I was doing this in person, this is about the time she'd start throwing things. She hangs up on me.

It takes me only a week to unwind seven years of momentum. I find that sad. It shouldn't be that easy. Maybe this is God making it easy for me. I abandon all my fears.

I'm on the plane to Raleigh now.

The idea of starting fresh takes root. This'll be great. I am a healed man. I am free of baggage. I can truly love a woman now. I have let go of my pain. I want a little house and a little dog, and when I wake up on weekend mornings I will not be restless. I will be so at peace that I can stay in bed for hours. I'll get a job at the Duke hospital and see patients. This will be my true place in life.

On the plane, three times I go into the bathroom to fool with my hair or change my shirt.

I walk off the plane into the boarding area, and . . .

Well, maybe she's waiting for me in the baggage claim area.

I go down to baggage claim, and . . .

Maybe she's stuck in traffic. I wait twenty minutes, until the last bag on the carousel is retrieved.

It starts to sink in. I'm in a strange town, I don't know a single person. I'm in a state in which the number one industry is pig farming and Jesse Helms is senator.

What the hell am I doing?

I have an address. Just get a cab, I'm sure everything's fine, there's just been a mix-up.

I get the cab. It all comes to me on the way. I'm freaking her out. I'm a strange man suddenly invading her turf, taking over her life. I'll be asking her to love me. I'll be asking her for directions to the supermarket. I'll be asking her to borrow her car. Who can love a man who needs them too much?

The cab lets me off in front of the address. It's a little single-story brick house. Jennifer answers the door. She's silent, torn, kisses me softly and wonderfully but not quite passionately.

Yup, I'm freaking her out.

"I thought you would pick me up at the airport," I let slip.

I shouldn't have said that.

She tours me through the house.

It is a little house. There are two bedrooms, and when she gets to the second bedroom she says, "This is your bedroom."

I just let that disappointment hang there.

"So you'll have your own space," she adds.

This isn't what it was supposed to be like.

—

You get Xerostomia from dead salivary glands. You get dead salivary glands from radiation therapy. You get radiotherapy for head and neck cancer. Thirty-nine thousand people each year get head and neck cancer. All get radiation. Fifty-eight percent get Xerostomia. Four out of five will die anyway. They all have a dying wish.

Seven years ago, a professor suggested I study the chemical Ethyol, simply because little was known about it. I put Ethyol in petri dishes with every kind of cell or body tissue imaginable. Then I mixed Ethyol with other drugs and recorded what happened. It was merely trial and error. Six years ago, I noticed that Ethyol didn't degrade under radiation. I theorized that this chemical could, perhaps, block radiation if injected into the salivary glands. Five years ago, I formed a company and raised money. The body is a mystery; what works in a test tube won't necessarily work in humans. I'd never seen Xerostomia, only read about it, yet I became convinced I could prevent it. According to my peers, I made the leap of faith too soon. Doing so is my weakness. Ignoring warning signs, going on faith.

Four years ago, we settled on a safe dose. Three years ago, we began tests in humans. Two years ago, we began receiving reports of adverse events—Ethyol was a neurotoxin, directly causing nausea, vomiting, and dizziness. We considered abandoning the study or restarting it with a smaller dose. A year ago, we unblinded the data and found that Ethyol worked. Xerostomia was prevented. We saved no lives, but dying wishes were being granted.

The panel would not be impressed.

The FDA emphasizes the saving of lives, not the quality of life.

Quality of life only counts if you're going to live. According to the FDA, there is no such thing as quality of death. Hippocratic oath, et cetera.

Four out of five die anyway.

There was nothing in the data about dying wishes.

We had run one study in France and Germany. Something was lost in the translation. Doctors there had recorded many cases of "moderate" Xerostomia as "mild" Xerostomia. What was mild and what was moderate, anyway?

The FDA doesn't let you toss a study out simply because you don't like its data.

We tested Ethyol on eight hundred patients over four years on two continents. Six hundred nineteen of them died within six months, same as the control group.

I get one hour in front of the panel.

"I've got to find a way to get this across," I say in anguish as the hour approached.

"We're fine," Linda assures me.

"We're not fine."

"Why not?"

"Because it sounds like we're asking them to approve a poison for sale so that some people who are going to die anyway won't get cotton mouth."

"You're being cynical."

"It's a band-aid. It fixes nothing."

"The proper term is *palliative care*."

"We have to convince the panel we're not talking about a little cotton mouth."

"We have an overhead slide on milliliters of saliva production."

"No! No slides! I need someone to bear witness."

"Bear witness?"

"Yes. Bear witness."

"Cry their eyes out?"

"Exactly."

"This isn't some Disney movie. The panel won't appreciate being manipulated."

"It's my only chance."

What was the value of a dying wish?

What was the value of being able to say "I love you" one more time?

—

I've known Jennifer for two hours. We're having dinner. Dinner is hamburgers, and thick french fries that we dip into steak sauce, and beer in frosted mugs. It's nothing like a date. We're helplessly drawn to each other. I hang on every word she says. She's wearing brown stretch capri pants and sandals and a short-sleeved cashmere sweater under my corduroy coat. Her toenails are painted white. Her lipstick's umber. She has freckles. She's real and stunning at the same time. Her eyes hint at an incredible innate curiosity. We tell each other stories, get the nuance of each other's jokes, listen attentively without interrupting. We feel safe, so safe that we begin to confess everything we have to confess, trying to scare each other off, but what doesn't scare us off only makes us stronger. I tell her about Jo in Montreal and the three years of on-again, off-again attempts to find the sweet spot in that relationship. I tell her about my tendency to want to take care of women who don't need any taking care of. I tell her I will lie under pressure, the most ruinous habit of all. I tell her I drive women away by neglecting them because I'm afraid to confront the moment of truth.

"I can't hurt people." People? Why'd I say "people"? There's a little lie right there. *Women.* I can't hurt women. To the point that I destroy them with mazes of yeses and maybes.

None of it scares her. She tells me she's always had long-distance relationships. Her friends tell her she's the most independent woman they've ever met. She loses sexual attraction to men after sleeping with them for a month. Her dead father was a giant in her psyche. Her mother was jealous of her, still is. Et cetera. None of it scares me off. It's too soon to judge. I just listen, rapt.

We just keep doing this, trying to find reasons not to like each other.

It doesn't work.

Then she says, "Okay, I have a confession."

Here it comes.

"We've never met, but . . . we almost met."

Not once, but twice.

The first time, three years ago, Jennifer came to my lab as a journalist. I refused to meet with her, shunning the publicity. She sat outside my lab door for three hours. She figured me for a typical doctor-type megalomaniac. She hated me.

The second time, a year ago, the FDA convened a panel to discuss standardizing the measurement of quality of life. She came to report on it. I was going to speak. Two hours before the panel, she got a phone call from her stepmother that her father was in the hospital. Jennifer jumped on a plane to North Carolina.

The invisible hand of history kept pushing us together. Sooner or later we would meet. A blind date set up by God.

"What do you think this means?" I ask.

"I don't believe in these kinds of things."

"What kinds of things?"

"Soul mates. For every woman there is one right man, yada yada yada."

"Me neither," I lied.

"I don't try to find meaning in coincidence," she said, but it occurred to me she might be lying too.

The attraction between us is not an everyday attraction.

"You and I are just two people who met," she tries, but the characterization doesn't fit.

What if she is the one? I have only three days to find out.

Now I need to know everything about her. "Tell me more," I beg.

"More."

Thirty-six, never married but engaged twice, a middle child between two brothers, her mother a little schizophrenic, her father a polite boozer who sold commercial insurance. Grew up in the French Quarter of New Orleans, moved to Minnesota halfway through high school, teased for her accent but learned to speak softly and showcase her blond hair to fit in. A year into college, her father couldn't handle her mother's schizophrenia anymore, freaked out, met another woman, and cut his family off. Unable to afford tuition, Jenny dropped out. She refused to let resentment destroy her. She loved music, couldn't play a lick, so sent dispatches about concerts to the local weekly, which published them. Bands let her in. Music in the Twin Cities was exploding. She covered the scene for the *Chicago Tribune*. At thirty, she gave it up while she was still young enough to find something new. She did the bravest thing she could think of: She tracked down her father in North Carolina.

She survived a life of hurt, and the only scratch to show for it is she's still alone.

I've known her for half a day and already I'm thinking, Shit! Shit! I have to go to Montreal in two days.

She wants to know what it's like to be around so many people dying all the time.

"I'm a research doctor, not a clinician."

"No fair."

"What?"

"Answer the question."

All right. It is a dark master, perversely supple in its slaveries, adept in its addictions. It makes the heart a knot that only gets tighter when I try to unwind it.

"Don't be cryptic," she insists.

"I keep people at a distance," I say.

But I can't seem to keep her at a distance. The knot is loosening.

We make love holding hands, looking into each other's open eyes, chest to chest. Sensation comes from everywhere, from my thighs on her thighs, my feet wrapped in her feet.

"I don't do this on first dates," she feels the need to tell me.

"It's only because we have so little time," I say.

She rolls on top and asks me to lie still so she can kiss on me. I can't do it. I have to be reciprocating. She kisses my chest. I try to massage her foot, but she slaps my hand away.

"Just lie still, honey."

I can't. I can't. I can't.

She drapes the ends of her hair over my belly.

Now I really can't. Oh god.

"Just lie still, baby."

Now I'm starting to cry. She's being too nice to me. I can't take it. I'm groaning and moaning and practically hyperventilating. She's being too soft, too nice.

She just keeps her tongue on my belly, right under my ribs, just this side of tickling me, just that side of taking a bite out of me. Oh god.

"Do you do this to every man?"

"I've never done this before in my life."

I'm a horse being broken. Five, ten minutes, until I finally can just lie there and let her touch me. She puts my arms over my head and runs her fingers through my armpits until I stop jerking. I'm a new man. I'm ruined for other women.

"Now let's do it right," she says, and I find out what she means.

I look at the clock. Three hours just went by. Time stands still. We're lying there, she's stroking down my damp sweaty hair, kissing my shoulder. We're going to lie here all night.

She says, "My father was in your trial."

—

The next morning I tell Linda I'm thinking of not going to Montreal.

"But your work—"

"Seven years is enough."

"Take a vacation."

"I met a woman."

"Bring her to Montreal."

"Jo is there."

"So?"

"We were going to move in together."

"So don't."

"I can't even imagine telling Jo."

"You'll have to tell her."

No. It's unimaginable. I will never, ever be able to let her down like that.

"Who is this woman?"

I mention Jennifer walking down the hall yesterday.

"Her! Her! You just met her yesterday! You don't give up your life's work for a woman you met yesterday!"

"I think she's wonderful."

"Are you crazy!?"

"I've never felt like this."

Linda rips into me. I'm a stupid jackass with blinders on. Can't I see that I'm just vulnerable right now because seven years of work is coming to a head? Can't I see that I'm afraid of failing and just looking for something else to hope for? Can't I see that I'm entertaining thoughts of throwing my life away to prepare for the possibility that the panel will reject my application? No woman has cracked me open. My work has cracked me open, and the first woman to just walk down the hall fell into the crevasse.

I bring up my intuition. This is a big mistake. Intuition = wish fulfillment, in Linda's book. I'm just scared of what'll happen with Jo.

Linda brings me to my senses.

"We've got a presentation to make tomorrow," she says. "Let's get focused."

We spend several hours on spinning the results of the European trial, where what is mild and what is moderate was lost in the translation. Too many patients from this column ended up in that column.

On that alone, I'll lose the vote of Dr. Victor Santana, who's a stickler for statistics.

I've already lost the vote of Robert Ozols, who could care less about quality of death.

And Krook and Nerenstone usually vote with Ozols.

That's four votes. I lose two more and my application will be denied.

What is mild and what is moderate? That's all I'm thinking about.

But that's not a connection a man can forget.

I start thinking about Jennifer. I haven't slept and I'm a little hallucinatory.

"Do we have those big red patient binders?" I ask Linda.

"In the boxes," she says.

"Will you look up a patient?"

"Which trial?"

"Thirty–forty-nine."

She goes to the box. We're eating little turkey sandwiches brought in by the hotel caterer and drinking ginger ale we snuck in from the drugstore. The room smells like dry-erase marker.

"Which patient?"

"Last name Boudreaux. That's e-a-u-x."

"Phillip?"

"That's the one."

"Died 8/6/99, age sixty-four. Test site was Duke."

"Did he get Ethyol?"

"He was in the control group."

"Xerostomia?"

"Severe."

—

I've been in Montreal a week now.

I keep seeing Jennifer in crowds. Jo takes me to Trudi, an incredible restaurant in the gay part of town. The meal's incredible. There's truffle oil in everything. On a warm night like this, Montreal is Europe in the best of ways. I haven't heard English for hours. Everyone's clothing is skin-tight. We hail a taxi back to her flat.

It's been a week, and she's earned the right to ask if I'm making a commitment here.

Everything I can say is the wrong answer.

When she looks in my eyes she can see the wrong answer, right there, plain as day.

I ask for some time. I'm new to town, a little culture-shocked, et cetera.

She tells me that in the real world, you don't get to make things wait. If your kid gets sick, you can't say "This isn't a good time right now." If you get in a car accident, you can't say "Hold on, I have to deal with some issues."

She's right. She's right. But I just need a little time.

"Whatever you're dealing with, you have to deal with it and love me at the same time," she says. "Whatever it is, I don't care. Just don't stop loving me."

She needs me to make love to her. She's thinking, If we just make love, he'll remember or he'll wake up from this and it'll all be fine.

We lie in bed with the window open, listening to the car alarms.

"You're going to be fine, sweetie," she says.

"I'm going to get better. It's just going to take me a while."

"I know."

———

I've been in North Carolina for six weeks.

I took the first job offered to me in order to look strong and independent to Jennifer. I'm a vice president of clinical research for Bristol-Myers Squibb—there are six more layers of bureaucracy above me, and five below. I am thrown onto a team overseeing the development of a protein that we hope will regrow cartilage in worn-out knees. The trial is a mess; the MRI cross-sectionals are inconclusive. I'm in meetings all day long. I work from 7:30 a.m. to 6:00 p.m. to stay out of Jennifer's hair.

When we make love, everything is great again.

The rest of the time, it's almost love. Still.

I do her grocery shopping and she makes me Cajun meals from her childhood. She has me buy things I can't spell. *Melatons*. It's some sort of green squash. She asks for chives and I bring home chives and she asks "What's this?" and laughs at me. Those are chives. It turns out she means green onions, but she refuses to call them anything but chives. I adore her.

I never want the lovemaking to stop. Every other night, she needs to sleep alone. So after lovemaking I go into the second bedroom and sleep in the bed her daddy died in. She's not over it yet. Clearly.

I'll wait. I have to. I made my choice.

———

I've known her for three days. The plane to Montreal is in five hours. What do I do?

I wake up. Time has started again. I want to tell her I love her. Tell her, you fool. My mouth is sewn closed.

"What are we going to do?" she asks.

"I can see loving you," I say.

"I can see loving you, too."

It's not the same and we both know it. Now we cemented it.

"You really want me to bear witness?" she says.

"It could make a big difference."

"And if the drug is approved, you're going to Montreal?"

"My flight's in five hours."

"I'm going to give a speech that sends my lover to another woman."

"If it's a good speech."

She healed me. She taught me to love again. We shower, dress, go downstairs, share a bear claw.

"Tell me why quality of life can't be measured again?"

"It can be measured. But only in milliliters."

"How much time will I have?"

"Fifteen minutes."

I advise her that the two swing votes will be Kathy Albain, from Loyola University in Illinois, and Richard Simon, from the National Cancer Institute. Do not talk to them. Doctors don't like to be confronted. Pretend you're talking to the audience.

Seven years, fifteen minutes, two hundred million dollars.

At 9:30 we are called to order. Linda presents data on how quickly Ethyol is purged from the system. In other words, it poisons you, but not for too long. *The incidence of hypotension trends toward control in seventy-two hours.* . . . I present data on why a dose of this dangerous magnitude is nevertheless necessary to prevent long-term Xerostomia. *Half the patient population received radiation doses in excess of sixty-five hundred cycles.* . . . None of it matters. The panel's faces are blank.

We're talking quality of death.

You wake up. Your mouth has been sewn closed. You've swallowed a two-by-four. You can't talk.

What we mean when we say hypotension is, you pass out.

When I inject Ethyol into the salivary glands, radiotherapy kills the tumors but not the glands. You'll pass out off and on for three days and vomit for a week. But you'll be able to talk until you die anyway.

There are all these other cancers to study its use in: ovarian, rectal, colon.

Jennifer is up on the stand, sending me to another woman.

"My father was Richard Boudreaux, identified in the case files of trial 30–49 as patient number 005-513—

"He did not receive Ethyol—

"For the last two months of his life, my daddy could not talk—

"Every morning I'd come into his room and his eyes would plead with me—

"One time he tried to talk and he ripped the roof of his mouth off and had to receive twenty-two stitches—

"He spent the last two months of his life on the computer, writing me letters—

"He felt like there were all these things he never got to explain—

"Such as why he had to leave Mom—

"Or why my stepmother wanted him to cut us off—

"All he wanted was to be able to explain himself—

"He wrote these gorgeous letters—

"He signed them all, 'I'll carry my love for you to the other side, and it'll be waiting for you when you get there.'—

"I thought it was a lyric from a song, but I don't know which song. He died before he could tell me."

Richard Simon is unimpressed. Kathy Albain votes yes. Seven votes to approve, five against. Ninety-nine times out of a hundred, the FDA will accept the panel's recommendation.

—

I've been in Montreal a month now. I started working again. I'm injecting Ethyol into the lymph glands of ovarian cancer patients for a safety profile. Jo is a nurse in an organ-transplant center. I'm getting better. I found out how to love again. For a long time I couldn't find the romance in my relationship with Jo. It was too raw, always fighting, the long distance, the disappointments. When you fall in love, you're supposed to get a halcyon period. You're supposed to save up goodwill for the battles to come later. Even Jennifer and I got that for three days. With Jo, it's been a battle since day one.

And then one day Linda e-mailed me and asked me to tell her the story of my relationship with Jo. How did we end up together anyway?

I started writing it all down.

How I broke up her marriage. How I lost friends. How she was across the country. How we got in the car accident. How we broke up, got back together, broke up. There were other women in there, like Jennifer, and other men for her.

And Linda e-mailed back, "That's the most romantic story."

"It is?"

Until then, I didn't see it. We made it, despite all that.

Linda wrote, "If you two can make it through all that, I can definitely get over my boyfriend's snoring."

Sometimes I thank Jennifer for teaching me to let people get close again. I think there's a person inside all of us who's capable of great love. We're not as broken as we think.

—

I've known Jenny for three days, and the plane to Montreal leaves in an hour.

We're on the way to Dulles.

At check-in, I declare the drugs I'm carrying. Amifostine, Doxyrubicin, Paclitaxel. I get a long look from the agents.

"What you did was brave," I tell Jennifer.

"Are you going to get on that plane?"

"I think it's the right thing to do."

"You can come with me."

If it was love, I would.

"We just didn't have enough time," I say.

"Make time. Come with me."

"My work is too important. And I don't think you're ready for me. I'm kinda high-maintenance."

I get my boarding pass and we sit down at the Burger King for a last supper. We can't eat our cheeseburgers. We feed each other the french fries. She starts to cry, and I start to cry.

I give her my corduroy coat.

She says, "I can take you being with someone else. But just please, please, don't forget about me. That's all I want now. I just don't want to be forgotten."

You will never be forgotten.

I get on that plane.

About the Contributors

ERIC GARCIA is a twenty-eight-year-old writer from Miami whose novels include *Anonymous Rex, Casual Rex* (March 2001), and the forthcoming *Hot and Sweaty Rex*. He attended Cornell University and the University of Southern California, where he majored in creative writing and film. He currently lives outside Los Angeles with his wife, daughter, and chubby dachshund, and splits his writing time between novels and film/TV projects, slaving over a hot computer for eighteen hours a day with little time for food, water, or skinny-dipping. On the rare occasion that he is allowed by his editors at Random House to venture away from the home, he enjoys a good game of racquetball, or a nice pastrami on rye, whichever is closer. He can be reached on the Web at www.casualrex.com.

GARY KRIST is the author of two novels, *Chaos Theory* and *Bad Chemistry*, and two short-story collections, *The Garden State* and *Bone by Bone*. A recipient of the Stephen Crane Award and the Sue Kaufman Prize from the American Academy of Arts and Letters, he also writes regularly for *The New York Times, Salon, The Washington Post Book World*, and other publications. He lives in Chevy Chase, Maryland, with his wife and daughter, and can be reached via www.garykrist.com.

CHRIS OFFUTT is the author of *Out of the Woods, Kentucky Straight, The Same River Twice*, and *The Good Brother*. All have been translated into several languages. His work is widely anthologized and has received many honors, including a Guggenheim Fellowship and a Whiting Award. He currently lives in Iowa City, where he is a visiting professor at the Iowa Writers' Workshop.

DAVID LISS is the author of *A Conspiracy of Paper*. He is also a doctoral candidate in the Department of English at Columbia University, where his work centers on how the mid-eighteenth-century British novel reflects and shapes the emergence of the modern idea of personal finance. He has presented numerous talks on his work, published on Henry James, and received several awards, including the Columbia President's Fellowship, an A. W. Mellon Research Fellowship, and the Whiting Dissertation Fellowship. Liss grew up in south Florida, but escaped, and currently lives with his wife in New York City. He can be reached through his website, www.davidliss.com.

RICHARD DOOLING is a writer and a lawyer. His second novel, *White Man's Grave,* was a finalist for the National Book Award in fiction. He is also the author of *Critical Care, Blue Streak,* and *Brain Storm,* a novel. His work has appeared in *The New Yorker, Esquire, The New York Times, The Wall Street Journal,* and the *National Law Journal.* He lives in Omaha, Nebraska, with his wife and children. His next novel will be published by Random House. His website can be found at www.dooling.com.

BRUCE STERLING already has three women in his life (a wife and two daughters), not counting his agent and most any number of his editors and assistant editors. Bruce Sterling is not actively seeking any more women at the moment. He has every confidence they will show up entirely on their own, probably through e-mail. Bruce Sterling's home page is well.com/conf/mirrorshades/ where one can find, among many other digital goodies, a list of his fourteen books and his innumerable magazine articles.

PAUL HOND is the author of *The Baker.* He lives in New York, where he is currently at work on his second novel.

ROBERT ANTHONY SIEGEL's short fiction has appeared in *Story* magazine and on the website Nerve.com. His first novel, *All the Money in the World,* was published by Random House in 1997. He is a graduate of the Iowa Writers' Workshop and teaches fiction at New York University's School of Continuing Studies. He can be reached at rasiegel1000@aol.com.

ALEXANDER PARSONS grew up in Santa Fe, New Mexico. He attended the Iowa Writers' Workshop and New Mexico State University's Creative Writing Program. His first novel, *Leaving Disneyland,* won the 2000 Associated Writing Programs' Award for the Novel and is forthcoming from St. Martin's

Press. He is currently finishing his second book, *El Malpaís.* He can be contacted at nuevogato2000@yahoo.com.

PO BRONSON is the author of *The Nudist on the Late Shift* (1999), *The First $20 Million Is Always the Hardest* (1997), and *Bombardiers* (1995). He has also written for the television drama *The $treet* (2000), as well as for *The New York Times Magazine, The Wall Street Journal,* and *Wired.* Bronson grew up in Seattle, graduated from Stanford University in 1986, and lives in San Francisco. For more information, visit www.pobronson.com.

AtRandom.com books are original publications that make their first public appearance in the world as e-books, followed by a trade paperback edition. AtRandom.com books are timely and topical. They exploit new technologies, such as hyperlinks, multimedia enhancements, and sophisticated search functions. Most of all, they are consumer-powered, providing readers with choices about their reading experience.

AtRandom.com books are aimed at highly defined communities of motivated readers who want immediate access to substantive and artful writing on the various subjects that fascinate them.

Our list features literary journalism; fiction; investigative reporting; cultural criticism; short biographies of entertainers, athletes, moguls, and thinkers; examinations of technology and society; and practical advice. Whether written in a spirit of play or rigorous critique, these books possess a vitality and daring that new ways of publishing can aptly serve.

For information about AtRandom.com Books and to sign up for our e-newsletters, visit www.atrandom.com.